Shorty Hough felt a great sense of satisfaction. As soon as he had this bunch of men lined out, so scared they had to do what he told them, he'd run the once-mighty Van Horns right out of the country.

"Ain't but one thing to do," Shorty told them. "Pitch the body off the rim. Time they find him, they won't know whether he was shot or not."

Captain Tappan shuddered. Lew Warren's mouth was trembling at the corners. But Luke Bartram was grinning, as if this was something to be enjoyed. . . .

"Take your pick, boys," Shorty Hough said savagely. "Pitch him over or hang. Which is it goin' to be?"

TOMAHAWK

Lee Leighton

BALLANTINE BOOKS • NEW YORK

All rights reserved under International and Pan-American
Copyright Conventions. Published in the United States by
Ballantine Books, a division of Random House, Inc., New
York, and simultaneously in Canada by Random House of
Canada, Limited, Toronto, Canada.

Library of Congress Catalog Card Number: 58-8344

ISBN 0-345-29431-9

Manufactured in the United States of America

First Edition: March 1958
Fifth Printing: January 1981

First Canadian Printing: March 1958
Second Canadian Printing: February 1981

Tomahawk

One

An icy wind knifed out of the dark north sky and lifted, sighing, from the great, deep trough of Salt Creek Valley to the west. It howled among the towering spires of Cathedral Rim and whipped at the dusty clothes of Kirk Van Horn and the other two riders who had reined their horses to a halt at the edge of the precipitous rim atop the great plateau.

A single rider, another Tomahawk cowhand, galloped toward them from the east. When he reached them, he reined up, saying breathlessly, "Kirk, your ma's sick. Matt said to tell you to come home."

Fear took hold of Kirk, fear that was almost premonition. He'd been back on his home range for six months after being gone for five years, and during every day of those six months he had lived in dread of receiving the very news Frank Surrency had just brought him.

He nodded at Surrency, refusing to show his feelings. "All right." He glanced at the high, thin clouds that held promise of neither rain nor snow, then turned abruptly with a gesturing arm to the pair who were with him. "Work out that draw and come in."

His glance swung to Surrency. "Give them a hand, Frank, or it'll be way after dark before they finish."

They started to ride away, but he halted them with "Frank, you know what's wrong? Is she very sick?"

Surrency's face was grave. He said, "Matt looked scared. Said she was feverish yesterday and all last night. That's as much as I know. You go on home. We'll take care of this."

Kirk watched them ride down into the timbered draw toward the rim, their horses stirring clouds of dust from the chalk-dry grass. Then he turned and rode away.

He was a tall young man who showed more of his mother's fine-boned refinement than his father's ponderous strength. Strength was there, though it was more the supple strength of a whip than that of a club.

His face was lean, almost thin, browned by sun and

chapped by the raw April wind. His eyes were gray, and had a way of softening with humor which did not always extend to his mouth. When they did, the skin at their corners would gather in dozens of tiny crow's feet. His mouth was long and straight, firm-lipped above a determined chin, which, because he'd been on roundup for over a week, was covered by a heavy brown stubble.

He lifted his horse to an easy canter, heading toward the Tomahawk buildings on Beaver Creek by way of the cow-camp which served as headquarters for spring roundup on this section of Tomahawk range. As he rode, he thought about the quarrels he'd had with his father, the unnecessary beatings, and how he'd finally left home when he was eighteen because he couldn't stand it any longer.

At the moment he was working for his father whose Tomahawk was the biggest outfit in the country, but only during spring roundup. Actually he didn't need to work for anyone else. When he'd come back, he'd bought the K Bar, a small spread on Salt Creek that provided all he needed.

Kirk probably would not have returned at all if his mother's letters had not created in him the fear that she wasn't well, fear that had been justified when he'd come back and seen her—too frail for a woman in her early forties. He wouldn't be riding for Tomahawk now, either, if his mother hadn't asked him to try again. So he'd swallowed his pride, and now he was glad that he had.

He put these thoughts out of his mind. From habit, his gaze moved ceaselessly over the landscape. He saw a deer, horns mere knobs of velvet, leap the five-wire fence that separated Buck Point from Tomahawk. He frowned, forgetting the animal as it disappeared into the brush.

At this place the difference between Buck Point and Tomahawk range was graphically illustrated. On the Tomahawk side of the fence, dry grass left over from last year was abundant and heavy, but Buck Point, which was summer graze for the small Salt Creek outfits, including Kirk's K Bar, had been overstocked so that if a man didn't know better he'd have said it was sheep range.

A worried gravity came to Kirk's eyes. If the rain didn't come . . . if the drought wasn't broken soon. . . .

He shook his head angrily and angled away from the fence.

8

Half an hour later he reached Tomahawk's roundup camp and put his horse down the slope to the corral.

He changed horses quickly, his eyes missing neither the thin plume of smoke whipping away from the tin chimney nor the trio of 3Y horses which stood ground-tied between corral and cabin. 3Y belonged to Eli Yockey, who, by virtue of owning the biggest outfit on Salt Creek, was the accepted leader of the small ranchers there.

The visitors came out of the cabin, having heard Kirk ride up, and stood in a group, waiting. Kirk's glance ran over the three as he approached, leading his horse. Eli Yockey shambled toward him, arm outstretched. Kirk took it, mildly surprised as he always was at the way Eli's great hand enveloped his own.

Eli's shoulders were broad and sloping, his brown eyes tiny and close-set. His hair, which should have been gray, was black as shoe polish. Kirk suppressed a grin at the comparison, having heard that Eli did indeed dye his hair with shoe polish to hide the encroachments of age.

Kirk's gaze moved past Eli to the trim form of his daughter Rachel. She was a handsome woman, full-bodied under the jeans and faded blue shirt she was wearing. She smiled at him warmly. Kirk returned her smile, stirred by her as he always was. She was an exciting girl, and she made no secret of her feeling for him.

Shorty Hough, the third member of the party, stood apart from the Yockeys, scowling at Kirk. He was Eli's one-man crew, and claimed to be the equal of any other three men on Salt Creek. During roundup he came close to making his brag good. He was squat and stocky, with tremendous strength in his great arms, and now, seeing the way Rachel Yockey looked at Kirk, his broad face grew hard with his jealousy.

Kirk said, "Howdy, Eli—Rachel." He nodded at Shorty, impatient to be gone, but he liked both Eli and Rachel, and would not offend them by being brusque.

Eli grinned uneasily. He shifted on his feet the way a bear might while eyeing a wild honey tree, thinking both of the honey's sweetness and the pain of the bees' stings. He cleared his throat and said, "Man, it's dry. You seen the grass on Buck Point lately?"

Kirk laughed. "What grass, Eli?"

9

Eli nodded. "That's what I mean." He cleared his throat, and added, "Plenty of dry grass left over from last year on Tomahawk range."

He couldn't come out and make a direct request; he had his pride and Kirk understood it. Bad feeling between Eli Yockey and Guy Van Horn had gone back almost as long as Kirk could remember. He asked, "What do you want, Eli? Grass?"

Eli's eyes were grateful. "Why yes, that's why we're here. Us Salt Creek folks want to lease summer range from Tomahawk. We had a meetin' just after you came up here to work roundup for your pa. We figured to pay two-bits a head for the summer, and thought we'd see you first since you're kind of one of us . . ."

Kirk glanced at Rachel, the phrase "kind of one of us" echoing in his mind. His glance slid on to Shorty who was still glaring at him, and returned to Eli. He knew how it was with people on Salt Creek. Aside from the personal bitterness between Eli and Kirk's father, there was the natural animosity that poor men feel toward a rich and powerful neighbor. From the day Kirk had bought the K Bar, he knew that the others on Salt Creek had not forgotten he was Guy Van Horn's son.

Kirk's inclination would have been to say yes to Eli's request, but he knew his father. Guy would never honor an agreement made by anyone but himself.

"I can't promise anything," Kirk said, "but I'll put it up to Guy and let you know."

Eli's eyes brightened, for he considered the battle half won with Kirk on his side, but Shorty muttered, " 'I'll ask Guy', he says. Hell, he's got to go to Guy every time he wants his nose blowed."

Eli swung around angrily, "Shut up, Shorty."

"I told you this was a fool stunt," Shorty said, his tone openly defiant. "Guy Van Horn wouldn't give you this . . ."

"Shut up!"

Shorty's mouth closed like a trap, his face sullen.

Rachel stepped forward and put a small hand on Kirk's arm, asking, "Are you coming to the dance at Salt Creek schoolhouse tomorrow night, Kirk?"

"Depends on how Ma is," he answered. "She's sick."

"Oh, I'm sorry. Is she bad?"

"I don't know. I was just going home to find out."

She moved closer, her head tipped back. "Please come if you can, Kirk."

He found it hard to resist her when she looked at him like that. He had often wondered if he should ask her to marry him, for she was in his thoughts much of the time. If he had a little more money, or a bigger spread . . .

"I'll come if I can, Rachel," he said, and turning to his horse, mounted. "I'll ask Guy soon as I get a chance, Eli, but you know how he is."

Shorty stood with his legs spread, his face still mirroring his hostility toward Kirk. As Kirk rode away, he heard Shorty and Eli arguing about the wisdom of asking the Van Horns for anything.

Kirk wondered about the change that had come over Shorty. At first meeting, the man had seemed good-natured and Kirk had liked him well enough. But that had been before Kirk started dropping around to see Rachel and taking her to the dances.

He'd heard that before he came back, Rachel had been going to the dances with Shorty, so the man had probably taken too much for granted. Now, thinking back over what had just happened, Kirk wondered if he would have promised Eli to ask Guy about the grass if Rachel hadn't been there. Probably not, he decided, for he knew what Guy would say.

Kirk shook his head impatiently and lifted his fresh horse into a run to make up for lost time. He stared at the plateau stretching ahead, rolling and broad, and gradually decreasing in elevation from the cliffs above Salt Creek where Cathedral Rim loomed a full twenty-five hundred feet above the valley to Beaver Creek which was flanked by low ridges that fingered westward toward the plateau.

It was ten miles from the cow camp to Tomahawk's headquarters ranch. The trail followed Red Creek which started as a spring at the cow camp and flowed into Beaver Creek a mile above the house, grown at that point to a respectable stream that even contained pan-size trout.

At times the sun was visible to Kirk through the overcast as a glowing, luminous ball that had neither heat nor much light. He rode through quakie pockets, through patches of

11

spruce and dense thickets of service-berry, across long flats covered only with sage and dry grass.

At sundown he reached a long, wide valley laced with irrigation ditches and plainly a hay meadow. In its center were two or three stacks of weathered wild hay, and at its far end there was a cabin built of graying logs.

Smoke rose from the chimney, filtering upward among the tall spruces which sheltered the cabin. It formed a blue haze which seemed to remain motionless, for here the thick growth of trees shielded it from the wind. This was the house of Delfino Chavez, who hunted wolves on Tomahawk range. Guy Van Horn paid him a bounty for each one that he killed and gave him this house where he lived with his daughter Bianca.

Kirk reined in before the door, calling, "Delfino!"

Bianca Chavez opened the door. She said, "He's inside, Kirk. Come on in."

Kirk stepped down, lifting a hand to her in greeting. There had been weariness in his face, weariness of body and discouragement of mind, but both faded as he looked at the girl.

Bianca was small and slender and active, yet her jeans and loose-fitting Mexican *camisa* failed to hide the fact that she was a woman and a very lovely one. Her hair was dark, with auburn lights glinting in it. Her eyes were the green of sage, her smile bright with genuine welcome.

Kirk batted his hat against his pants and grimaced at the cloud of dust he raised. He asked, "Think it'll ever rain again, Bee?"

She shook her head, studying him in a way both feminine and direct. She stepped aside to let him enter, but her eyes lingered on his face long after he had looked past her into the room. Her smile faded as she sensed the discouragement in him. Coming back to Tomahawk country had not been easy for him, and the future would not be any easier.

She moved past him, and reached for the graniteware coffeepot simmering on the back of the stove. Delfino, in his stocking feet, rose from a chair and extended a hand as brown and thin as cured rawhide. His eyes were sharp, icy green in a face as brown and thin as his hands. He wore a drooping mustache above a mouth that was long and with-

12

out much humor. Kirk had been far closer to Delfino when he'd been a boy than he had to his own father, and he still respected Delfino's judgment.

"How's the calf branding coming?" Delfino asked.

"All right." Kirk took a cup of coffee from Bianca and sipped it, standing. "When I stopped at the cow camp to get a fresh horse, Eli was waiting for me with Rachel and Shorty Hough. Eli and the rest of the Salt Creek bunch want grass. I couldn't promise 'em anything because I figure Guy will turn 'em down. What do you think they'll do if he does?"

"What'd they offer?"

"Two bits a head. It's fair enough, but Guy won't see it that way."

"No, he won't," Delfino agreed.

"You figure they'll make trouble?"

Delfino nodded. "I would if I had my tail in the same crack."

"You know 'em better'n I do. Who'll kick up the dust, Eli?"

Delfino pursed his lips. "Shorty Hough. He bristles like a stray dog every time you look at that Yockey filly. He'll make something out of it."

"He's got a right to," Bianca said sharply. "She used to be his girl."

Kirk took a chair at the table and set the coffee cup down in front of him. He lifted his gaze to Bianca. He noticed the way her eyes snapped, and wondered why she should take Shorty's side. Maybe a lot of people thought of Rachel as Shorty's girl, but the way she told it, she never had been.

In any case, Kirk didn't want to argue about it. He said, "Ma's sick, Bee. Could you come over for a couple of days? Think your old man can get along without you?"

The edge was instantly gone from her glance. "Sure he can." She smiled at Delfino. "He doesn't like my cooking anyway. He's eaten his own for so long while he's been out hunting wolves that he thinks he's the only one in the world who can cook."

Kirk finished his coffee in a couple of gulps and stood up. "Want me to saddle a horse for you?" he asked. "Or would you rather ride double the way you used to?"

She flushed, her eyes sparkling. Kirk laughed and backed

13

through the door, ducking with mock fright. Bianca stamped a foot angrily. He fled as she pretended to fling the empty coffeepot at him.

Bianca flounced into her bedroom for a coat. Her cheeks were high with color, her eyes bright. "Damn him! Damn him anyway."

She came out a moment later carrying a sheepskin and caught her father's amused eyes on her. She flared, "Don't laugh. Don't you *dare* laugh."

"I wasn't laughing."

"But you were looking."

He shrugged. "All right, I was looking."

She was contrite. "I'm sorry, Dad, but he makes me so doggone mad."

"I've seen lots of wolves like him, girl. Couldn't catch 'em—couldn't get close enough to kill 'em, either. Patience does the job. Patience, not temper."

She snapped, "He never even sees me. I might just as well be an old rock out there on the hillside."

Delfino grinned. "You should have ridden double with him."

"Maybe I should have," she said defiantly. "Maybe I'll even do more than that."

She ran out of the house, and Delfino heard her talking to Kirk as they mounted and rode away. From a distance he heard her laugh, bright, young, and full of life. His eyes grew warm with pride, then troubled as he thought of what Kirk had said about the Salt Creek bunch.

He had a feeling for trouble, did Delfino. He could feel it coming on as plainly as he could feel a change in the weather. And he felt it now.

Two

The sky was the color of slate as Kirk and Bianca broke from the timber into Tomahawk's wide-spread hay meadows. By this cold light they could see dozens of fenced stack-yards, each containing from one to six browned and weathered haystacks. They could see the blocky, dark red shapes of Tomahawk's Hereford bulls, pasturing and being fed here in the meadows awaiting the time when they could be turned out for the breeding season.

Yonder, by one of the stackyards, was a bullrake and a Mormon Derrick stacker. By another were two mowers and three or four dump rakes.

In the center of the vast system of fenced and cross-fenced meadows stood a cluster of buildings, dominated by a huge barn with its monstrous loft capable of holding fifty tons of loose wild hay. And nestling almost in the shadow of the barn was the house, impressively large in itself, but dwarfed by the barn.

Lamplight flickered weakly from the windows of the kitchen, from those of the great front room, so barren of livable furniture, and from an upstairs bedroom. Otherwise the house was dark.

The ground of the meadow was powdery under their horses' hoofs and the wind raised eddies of dust as they passed. When they reached the pole gate, Kirk opened it without dismounting, rode through and then held it back for Bianca. Still without dismounting, he closed it and shot the bar home.

They rode across the yard, now a maelstrom of dust stirred up by the increasing blast of wind. Kirk glanced at the house, thinking about his mother. She couldn't be too seriously ill, he thought with relief, or Doc Peters' buckboard would surely be here in the yard.

Bianca's horse shied suddenly, and Kirk said sharply, "Get down, Bianca, before you get bucked off! That horse of yours smells the bear."

She slipped off just in time. Her horse seized his head and bucked across the yard, leaving her standing alone in the growing darkness and whirling dust.

Kirk chuckled, and riding after the horse, brought him back. Dismounting, he led the two horses to the barn, took them inside, and offsaddled. He put the animals in different stalls, grained them, then turned to Bianca standing in the door.

He could hear the bear's soft whoofing outside the barn.

15

He said, "That bear, Eli, almost forgot me in the five years I was gone. But he remembers me now. I'll show you."

He led the way through the gathering darkness, careful to approach from upwind. After several moments he saw the bear's bulk before him and heard the rattling of the chain.

Eli, a seven-year-old brown bear, stood up on his hind legs as Kirk came within reach, towering this way almost as tall as Kirk himself. He dropped immediately to all fours and Kirk scratched his head while the bear tried to lick his hand.

Kirk grinned. "That's not all affection, Bee. Sometimes I have sugar in my hand."

Eli stood up again and shambled back and forth in front of them. Kirk chuckled. "See why we named him Eli? Sometimes when I see Eli Yockey walking along the street, I catch myself listening for the rattle of a chain."

Bianca said, gently reproving, "Kirk."

"Well, they do walk alike." Kirk grinned. "I've gotten so that when I pet the bear I find myself wondering if I'm going to get shoe polish on my hand."

Bianca giggled, then sobered. "I'm going into the house and see how your mother is."

She disappeared into the darkness. Kirk scratched the bear that was on all fours beside him. His hand encountered a raw, rubbed place on Eli's neck where the chain collar had chafed, and the bear growled softly with pain.

It was a wonder, Kirk thought, that Guy Van Horn had put up with the bear as long as he had, one of the few concessions he had ever made to his boys. Kirk remembered his father's threat, uttered often through the years: "I'll never turn that damn' bear loose to prey on my stock! He ain't scared of men the way a bear ought to be, and he sure likes the taste of beef. You kids better keep him on that chain or I'll hunt him down and kill him. Reckon I'll have to kill him anyway, soon's he grows up."

Kirk smiled grimly. Everything remained the same for Guy, whether from blindness or sheer stubbornness, Kirk didn't know. Guy refused to admit that two of his sons were grown. He didn't realize, either, that the bear was full grown. Maybe it was time he did.

16

Impulsively, Kirk's fingers fumbled with the catch on Eli's chain collar. He unfastened it and let it drop away. Eli sat down like a dog and scratched his neck with a hind foot where the chain had chafed. Then he stood up, apparently puzzling over the absence of the chain.

"You poor devil," Kirk muttered. "You're like Matt's going to be if he ever gets Pa's chain off his neck. You haven't got the least idea what to do with yourself because you never learned how a grown bear is supposed to act."

Kirk walked away, heading toward the house. The bear followed for a few feet until he seemed to realize he'd gone beyond the limits of the chain. He sat down and looked back.

"Go on, Eli," Kirk said angrily. "Get out of here. It's time you learned to act like a wild bear for a change."

As though understanding his words, Eli got up and shuffled away into the darkness. Kirk, suddenly and unaccountably ashamed, swore at himself. Never, as long as he lived, would he catch another wild thing and chain it up.

He tramped to the house, puzzled at himself and vaguely realizing that releasing Eli had been symbolic of his own restlessness and revolt that had not been satisfied by having his spread on Salt Creek. Then, as he entered the house, concern for his mother blotted out all other thoughts, for the faces of his brothers were pale and frightened.

The younger Van Horn boys were as unlike as Kirk's father and mother themselves. Matt, barely twenty-one, favored his father and was broad and thick through the shoulders, heavy-browed and long-jawed. The resemblance was only a superficial one, for he had neither the air of competence that was so much a part of Guy Van Horn, nor his ruthlessly demanding nature which had steadily grown more dominating through the years, nurtured as it was by a lifetime of riding roughshod over the rights and pride of both his neighbors and his sons.

Billy, who was fifteen, looked like a younger, quick-sprouting version of Kirk. Already he had something of Kirk's quiet manner and calm strength.

But there was another difference between Billy and Matt, one that went deeper than the physical one, a difference of spirit rather than body. Matt was already broken. Billy

17

wasn't. For that reason Kirk turned his gaze to Billy when he asked, "How is she?"

Both brothers were silent. Billy's eyes shifted. Matt scuffed his boots against the worn wood floor.

Kirk said, "From the looks on your faces I'd say she was damned sick. How soon's Doc going to get here?"

Matt cleared his throat. "Won't be for a while yet. We didn't send for him till after dinner."

Feeling a stir of both anger and panic, Kirk demanded, "Why didn't you send for him this morning?"

"Ma wouldn't let us," Matt answered. "She said Pa . . ."

Kirk followed Matt's excuses with only part of his mind, for he knew what they would be before he ever heard them. It was an old, familiar pattern by which the Van Horn family had always lived. The pattern was one of the reasons Kirk had left home five years ago. Matt and Billy had listened to their mother, who hadn't wanted them to send for the doctor. They had obeyed because they were afraid of Guy, who was thrifty to the point of niggardliness, so they had waited, unable to consult him because he was somewhere on Tomahawk range overseeing calf branding. Even Kirk didn't know exactly where he was.

Kirk was furious when he left the room. Tonight the lack of furniture in the huge, bare living room angered him inordinately. He scowled as he thought about it. It was so typical of Guy. He effected a double saving this way: it made unnecessary an expenditure for furniture and also gave him a storeroom, saving him the expense of building one.

Kirk climbed the narrow stairway two steps at a time, and strode along the hall toward the square of light shining through his mother's partly opened door. The instant he entered the room, he knew that her condition was serious. Her face was flushed with fever, and her eyes were closed despite Bianca's presence. Her thin chest rose and fell quickly with her breathing, which was as noisy as the rasp of a file on a horse's hoof.

Bianca had drawn a chair close to the bed and was sitting there, her face very pale. She rose when she heard Kirk, and motioned for him to step back into the hall.

"I'm scared, Kirk," she whispered.

He looked down at Bianca in the almost non-existent light

18

in the hall. Bianca was a hardhead, practical girl, and not one to give way to terror unless there was a real reason for it.

"The doc will be here before long," Kirk said.

"He should be here now," Bianca said bitterly. "It's all because of your father. Someday I'm going to tell him what I think of him."

She would, too, Kirk thought, and when she did, she'd do it up brown. Both Bianca and Delfino understood how it was with Guy, but understanding did not give them sympathy for him. Different from others who owed their living to Tomahawk, they weren't afraid of him. Wolfers like Delfino were rare and priceless in a wolf-ridden country like this, and Guy knew it.

"I'll sit with her for a while," Kirk said. "Go downstairs and get yourself a cup of coffee."

Bianca hesitated, her eyes on him, then she nodded and obeyed. Kirk returned to the bedroom and sat down beside the bed. His mother stirred and opening her eyes, looked at him. He realized at once that, sick as she was, she was perfectly rational.

"I'm glad you're here, Kirk," she whispered hoarsely. "I was afraid you wouldn't come in time."

He said gently, "Don't talk like that, Ma. All you need is a long rest."

She smiled very faintly. "I'm going to get a long rest, Kirk. But it's all right. I'm not afraid."

What could he say? She knew. And she wasn't afraid. If there was anything to this life after death business, he thought, she had no reason to fear. The best of it would be reserved for her.

He sat looking at her thin face with its deep lines. Lines that had been carved there by the harshness of hard work and worry and doing without, doing without for which there had been no real reason for many years.

Her thin hand came out and found Kirk's. "I'm so glad you came back. I didn't want you to leave, but I could see it was the best thing. You couldn't get along with your father and it would have gotten worse if you'd stayed. You're strong now, and you're a good man. You've gone the second mile, the hardest one, since you've come home. You've learned to live with your father."

She had gone the second mile, too, Kirk thought. She must have gone her second mile more than twenty years ago when she'd first married Guy. But she was wrong about one thing. He hadn't learned to live with his father.

"I've had a feeling I wasn't going to live much longer for quite a while," she went on. "It's why I wrote and asked you to come home." She smiled again faintly. "I won't worry about you, Kirk. You're grown and a man. It's Matt and Billy who worry me. Help them, Kirk. Help them all you can."

He said earnestly, "I will, Ma. I promise."

For a time she lay with the side of her face on the pillow watching him. Then she said, "I'm mortal tired, Kirk. I just don't have any strength."

Presently she closed her eyes and there was no sound in the room except the heavy sawing of her breath. It would be a miracle, he thought, if she were alive at sunup.

Bianca returned, carrying a pan filled with cool water, and a wash cloth. Kirk rose to let her have the chair. He asked her tightly, "Isn't there anything we can do?"

"I'm going to bathe her face and arms. I don't know of anything else I can do. If only the doctor was here."

That brought Kirk's thoughts again to his father. He left the room and walked wearily along the hall and down the stairs, wondering if Guy Van Horn would ever know how heavily the responsibility for this rested on his shoulders.

Three

The night dragged on with maddening slowness. Kirk paced the huge living room, too restless to remain motionless as Matt was. He made a path through the high-stacked piles of hundred pound sugar sacks, the barrels of flour, the kegs of nails and whisky, the awkward, wire-tied bundles of new haying machinery.

He barked his shin twice on the cutter bar of a mower. The second time he cursed savagely and kicked out with such force that he moved the cutter bar from his path.

Matt sat on a flour barrel watching him uneasily but with admiration in his eyes. Once or twice Matt cleared his throat as if intending to say something, but he remained silent. Kirk knew what his brother wanted to say. He had to explain his failure to send for the doctor when he had first known his mother was so sick; he had to justify himself and thus somehow still the gnawing fear that ate away at his insides.

At last Kirk said, "Don't keep on kicking yourself, Matt. Ma's going to be all right." He was lying, but he felt compelled to say it.

Matt nodded, though it was plain that the words did not relieve his feeling of guilt. Finally he said, "Kirk, you know how it is. He keeps treating me like a little kid and damn if I don't keep acting like one. But I've got to the end of my string." His lips tightened until they were white from the pressure. "I'm going to pull out."

Kirk studied him. The clock on the mantle chimed two. Kirk said, "Yeah, that's what you ought to do, Matt." But he knew his brother wouldn't do it when the time came. Matt had made this same resolve before and his determination had always fizzled out when he confronted Guy.

Depression settled on Kirk. He could hear Bianca's light footsteps on the floor overhead and was thankful she was here. There were things a woman could do in a sick room that a man was not capable of doing—little comforting things born of a woman's pity and understanding.

He let his thoughts linger on Bianca, wondering at her alternate moods of volatile anger and tenderness. Then he heard the rattle of a buckboard in the yard and nodded at Matt. "That's the doc now. Go put his team away."

He opened the front door and called, "Come on in, Doc. Matt will take care of your horses."

Matt went out, and a moment later Doc Peters stepped into the finger of light that fell past Kirk onto the bare yard in front of the porch. He was a pot-bellied man with a black spade beard and the kind face of one who placed the welfare of his patients above his own comfort. Kirk had never known him to turn down a call regardless of distance or weather.

The doctor stopped, his black bag in his hand, and looked

up at Kirk. "Your ma must be pretty sick to have me come to her instead of her coming to me."

"She's damned sick," Kirk said.

He turned and led the way up the stairs to his mother's room, the doctor following. Bianca rose from where she had been sitting beside the bed, her face showing her relief. "I'm glad you're here, Doc. I didn't know what to do."

Kirk saw that his mother's condition had not changed. If anything, her breathing was harder than before. He went back downstairs, feeling that he'd only be in the way if he stayed in her room. Matt came in presently, looking inquiringly at Kirk who shook his head.

"I don't know, Matt," Kirk said. "Doc's with her. He'll know what to do."

They waited, Kirk glad that Billy had gone to bed and didn't know how bad their mother was. It was hard enough on him and Matt to sit here and know there was nothing they could do. Then he heard the pound of a horse's hoofs.

It was Guy. Kirk didn't have to see him or hear his voice to know. In coming home this time of morning, Guy was following an old and threadbare pattern. He wouldn't leave the cow camp where he was until dark, when the work had to stop, so he always arrived home in the middle of the night.

Kirk followed Guy's progress toward the house by the great, slamming noises he made with everything he did. First the creak of un-oiled hinges as Guy swung the barn door open and led his horse inside. Then the vicious slam as he went back outside. And now the bang of the kitchen door and the heavy tramp of his boots, the scrape and ring of his Spanish spurs upon the floor.

Kirk rose, but Matt remained motionless, trying to look inconspicuous. Guy Van Horn stomped in, a great, wide-bodied man with a chest and belly like an oak barrel. He scowled, eyes moving from Kirk to Matt and back again. When he spoke, his voice was a rumble coming from deep in his throat.

"What the hell's Doc doing here this time of night?"

"Ma's sick," Kirk said.

"She ain't that sick! She can't be."

Guy strode toward Kirk and stood close, dwarfing him by

a couple of inches and outweighing him by fifty pounds. Kirk met his glare steadily, refusing to retreat. He said, "She is that sick. You'd better be glad Matt sent for Doc. I don't think she's going to make it."

A spasm like pain twisted Guy Van Horn's face. For the briefest instant Kirk saw torment in his eyes, then he looked past him to Bianca who was standing at the foot of the stairs with a lamp in her hands. He asked, "What does Doc think, Bee?"

"He got here too late," she said. "You'd better go upstairs, Mr. Van Horn."

Guy whirled on her, still not believing, but he must have seen something in her face that told him it was true. He brushed past her and stomped up the stairs.

Kirk glanced at Matt. His brother had an expression of abject fear on his face. When he realized Kirk was looking at him, he made a sickly grin. He'd been afraid Guy would blow up because he'd sent for the doctor.

Bianca came to Kirk and took his arm in both her hands. There was a tightness of desperation in her grip as though right now she needed something very solid to hang onto.

Overhead the beat of Guy's footsteps halted, and the rumble of his voice began. Then this, too, stopped, and a full minute passed with the silence complete and terrifying. The sound Kirk heard then was one he had never heard before, the sound of his father weeping, a sound he had never expected to hear from this implacably harsh man.

Kirk looked down into Bianca's face. It was white and bloodless, and her eyes were full of compassion, whether for him or his father he couldn't tell. The expression reminded him of his mother in the years that were past.

Kirk heard his father's heavy tread upon the stairs. He glanced up and saw Guy descending. The doctor, carrying his black bag, was a couple of steps behind. Kirk started toward his father, but a quality of expression on the older man's face made him stop. It was too late now—too late to go up again.

Guy's face was the face of a beaten man, yet behind the defeat was a kind of compensating fury. His eyes were bloodshot. He had faced an enemy he could not beat. Now he

23

seemed to be searching for some tangible enemy to take the place of death.

Though Kirk saw his father's grief, no sympathy stirred in him. He thought bitterly, *Look around you, Pa. Look for someone to blame.*

Doc Peters had stopped and was staring at Guy. He said, "You knew she wasn't well. The last time she came to town to see me, I told her to have you hire help for her."

"She didn't tell me," Guy said.

"And why didn't she?" the doctor asked. "Because she was afraid to! Afraid you'd rant about her spending money she didn't need to, so she kept on working when she shouldn't have. If you'd taken care of her like you should have . . ."

"Get out," Guy said harshly. "Get to hell out of here."

"I'll be glad to," Peters said, "but I'll be back for the funeral."

He walked out of the house, stiff-backed and angry. Matt scurried after him to help with his team. Guy didn't move from where he stood in the middle of the room. Kirk walked toward him. He gave Guy a steady look, then passed him and slowly climbed the stairs, Bianca following.

Guy Van Horn opened his mouth to call Kirk back, overcome all at once with a memory of another time when his wife had been sick and Kirk had been a small boy. They had comforted each other then, with Guy sitting in a big, leather-covered chair, and Kirk sobbing brokenly in his arms.

He walked around the room until he heard the sound of the doctor's buckboard leaving, then Matt came in, crying unashamedly much the same way Kirk had cried that day years ago. Guy took a step toward Matt, stopping as he realized for the first time that Matt and Kirk were no longer boys. They were men grown.

He remembered with aching regret how close he had been to both of them when they were small. The fury that had been in him a few minutes before over the doctor's accusation of neglect had burned out. The ashes that remained were only his questions about his sons. What Doc Peters thought meant nothing. When had things changed with his boys? When had the closeness disappeared?

He supposed it had been a gradual process, aggravated

by his inability to realize that boys become men by gradual stages and not all at once.

He knew he was the richest, most powerful cattleman between the Grand and the Yampa. Tomahawk was the biggest cow outfit within a hundred miles. Guy's face twisted with memory, the memory of how he had liked to brag that he had never been given anything. He'd earned everything he had and owed nothing to anyone.

He turned his head to look up the empty stairway, knowing now how wrong he had been. He felt a sudden, overpowering sense of loss, and for the first time in his life tasted the bitterness of self blame. He had owed his wife more than he had realized and knew now that he would miss her far more than he had thought he could ever miss anyone.

He remembered the day he had brought her south by stage from Rawlins to Jubilee on White River, then to this spot on horseback, and had begun building their first cabin. His throat ached with the memory of her beauty, her young freshness. He frowned, wondering where it had gone. It had slipped away gradually, he supposed, as had his sons' childhood, its going neither missed during the years of hard work that had gone into building Tomahawk, nor even fully realized.

Kirk came down the stairs. He stared at his father as though seeking something, but apparently he didn't find it. He said coldly, "Pa, I came back to this country because Ma begged me to. Now I'm leaving again. I'll be here for the funeral, but that's all." He swallowed. "Doc was right. You trained Ma well."

He took a deep breath and went on, "You know what Ma did day before yesterday? She cooked three meals for five men. She did a washing and hung it out herself in this cold wind. Yesterday she fussed all day because she couldn't get out of bed and work. And you with ten thousand cattle under the Tomahawk iron and a hundred thousand dollars in cash."

Guy stared at Kirk, making no effort to defend himself. His son's words hit him with shocking impact. Later their pain would be felt. Now there was only numbness.

Kirk took another long breath, then he went on more

sanely, "Maybe I won't get another chance to tell you, so I'll do it now. Eli Yockey and the other Salt Creekers want to lease range for the summer at two bits a head. I'd advise you to take it. There'll be trouble if you don't."

Guy's stunned mind seized upon this as an opportunity to vent the rage that had been dammed up too long. He said harshly, "How many times have I got to drum it into your thick head that I run Tomahawk? You made some kind of trade with that trash down there, didn't you? Or are you up to something with that fancy Yockey piece? Did old Eli catch you with her out in the brush?"

Kirk's hands opened wide, then closed and clenched until his knuckles were white. He was silent a long moment, then he said, his voice surprisingly calm, "Pa, they need grass. Buck Point looks like sheep range. The whole bunch will be broke before the summer's over if you don't give them grass—or they'll take it, which will be a damn sight worse."

Guy laughed. "Nobody takes anything from Guy Van Horn. Remember that while you're running with that pack of mangy coyotes down on Salt Creek. Remember it."

But even as he said the words, he knew they weren't true. Death had taken something from him tonight, something more precious to him than all of Tomahawk.

Pain was suddenly intolerable. He had never realized how dear she had been to him. And the worst of it was he'd never told her, had never even shown her by a gesture, how much she meant to him.

Without another word Kirk turned and went out of the room. Bianca who had just come down the stairs followed him. Matt remained where he was on a flour barrel, watching his father with fear in his eyes.

Four

The air outside was cold with pre-dawn chill. Kirk shut the front door. Bianca's face was a pale blur. She waited, and when Kirk had controlled the fury that was in him, he said,

"Bee, will you stay with her? I know it's a lot to ask, but . . ."

"Of course I'll stay with her. I loved her, too, Kirk."

He said, "I'll send Kate out from Jubilee to help."

"All right, Kirk."

He crossed the yard toward the corral. He roped a horse and saddled quickly. Matt hurried across the yard and into the corral with a rope in his hand. "I'm going with you, Kirk."

The sky was turning a cold gray in the east, but there was not enough light for Kirk to see his face. He asked, "Did you tell Pa you were going?"

Matt shook his head defiantly. "I can't face him down, Kirk. You know that. And I want to go."

Kirk shrugged, unwilling to make an issue of it now. He felt drained of all feeling, as though nothing really mattered any more. He'd get over it, but right now he didn't have much energy for arguing.

He waited impatiently until Matt finished saddling, then led out briskly toward the town of Jubilee, shivering in the cold dawn air. He took the horseback trail out across the rolling cedar hills of Tomahawk's winter range rather than the longer route by road down Beaver Creek and then up the White River. A couple of hours later he slid his horse off the bluff into the irrigated valley of the White River. The rising sun raised a haze from the valley floor that looked like smoke.

The town was a mile or more upriver, but here the ground was relatively level, and Kirk and Matt let their horses out. They covered the remaining distance in a few minutes, their horses running hard.

Kirk headed immediately toward Kate Gorman's house. Kate was an old friend of the family, having spent part of each summer for many years visiting at Tomahawk with Kirk's mother. Among his earliest memories was that of Kate's bluff competence. He knew she would take charge and make whatever arrangements were necessary for the funeral. Indeed, Kate would be hurt if she weren't asked to do so.

Matt hesitated at the picket gate. He said without meeting

27

Kirk's eyes, "Kirk, if I go in there, I'll bawl like a kid. I'll wait for you down at O'Mara's."

Kirk looked at him, wondering if Matt would ever act his years. He said, "All right, I'll see you there."

Matt rode away, and Kirk went up the walk to Kate's door. It was early, but he knew she had been up for hours. He knocked and she came to the door before he could repeat the knock.

She was a big woman in her mid-fifties, hearty and ample-bosomed. Her weathered face lighted when she saw him, and her huge, warm hand folded over his.

"Come in," she shouted. "Kirk, you rascal, how long's it been since you've been in town? Why, bless me, I'll bet I haven't seen you since the New Year's dance at the . . ." She stopped abruptly, her eyebrows raised at Kirk's expression. "What's wrong, boy?"

"Ma's gone, Kate. She died early this morning. I thought maybe you'd go out and make arrangements for the funeral. Bianca's there, but she'll need help." He still found it hard to realize his mother was dead. It seemed like a dream in the bright light of day. He added, "I just wouldn't know where to start."

Kate's eyes filled with tears, and her weathered face softened with compassion. Her big arms came out and folded Kirk against her breasts as she would have a little boy. He patted her a couple of times on the shoulder, then pulled away uncomfortably.

Kate dabbed at her eyes with the back of her hand and looked at him with keen wisdom. "Sorry, Kirk. Guy's made growing up a sore spot with you boys, hasn't he?"

Kirk didn't answer. Kate studied him for a moment. "There's more, Kirk. What is it?"

Kirk shrugged. "Same old thing. Pa."

Briskly she wiped her eyes with the hem of her apron. She kept twisting the apron between her hands, an automatic gesture that betrayed her agitation. She said the ancient words of woman trying to comfort a man's loss. "What you need is something to eat. Come on out to the kitchen."

Kirk opened his mouth to protest, but she cut him off impatiently. "Damn it, I'm not Guy, so get your hackles down."

Kirk couldn't help grinning any more than he could help

the warm feeling that spread through him. "Is your grub so bad you've got to scare folks into eating it?"

Kate grumbled something under her breath, but her eyes were pleased. She was profane and violent in her talk, a woman of strong opinions, and not overly popular in the small community of Jubilee because of it. But with those who understood her she found something she failed to find with the townspeople.

And Kirk did understand her—perhaps too well. He knew, for instance, that she was in love with Guy Van Horn, had been in love with him for years. He also knew she would rather die than have it known.

He wondered how she could love a man who repelled rather than attracted love, who apparently needed no one but himself and who had no thought for anything but Tomahawk. And yet Kate, next to Kirk's mother, should have known him better than anyone else, his good points and his bad ones. Kirk shrugged; there was no understanding a woman's love.

He followed her into the kitchen and ate the steak and potatoes and eggs she served him for breakfast. She watched him covertly throughout the meal. Finally she said, "You've been fighting with Guy again. What was it about this time?"

"What's it always been about?"

She nodded. "So you've left Tomahawk again?"

"I will, right after the funeral. I never got along with him and I never will."

Kate looked at him searchingly. "You're not very fond of yourself, are you, Kirk?"

"What do you mean?"

"You're turning your back on your home, boy, and Tomahawk means damn near as much to you as it does to Guy. You're turning your back on your brothers, too. That was why your ma wanted you to work roundup on Tomahawk, wasn't it, so you'd be with Matt and Billy?"

"I guess it was."

"I saw this coming years ago," Kate went on. "You were born with the seeds of rebellion in you that your ma, God rest her soul, didn't have. You don't feel quite right about walking off and leaving Tomahawk because you know Guy needs you, ornery as he is."

Kirk shook his head sourly. "I don't owe him anything."

Kate put her hands on her hips and glared at him. "You owe him plenty! What's more, your life's tied in with Tomahawk just as much as Guy's is. Every acre of that ranch has got your sweat on it just like it's got his. Some of them have got your pa's blood in them same as yours."

Irritated, Kirk rose and paced back and forth across the room. This wasn't what he wanted to hear. Kate's words had just enough truth in them to bother him.

"You know what eats on your pa?" When Kirk shook his head, she said, "I thought not. If you did, you could make some allowances for the ornery things he does. Not that they're right. They're not. But understanding helps."

She drew a great, gusty breath. "He was an orphan. A farmer back East took him out of an orphanage, raised him and worked him like a horse. To make him stay, the old booger promised him the farm when he died, saying he had no kin. Built the farm up, Guy did, doing the work alone 'cause by then the old man was poorly. The farmer died, and when the will was read, it said nothing about Guy—left the farm to some shirttail relative. Guy kicked up a ruckus. Upshot was he got evicted by the sheriff. When he put up a scrap, he got throwed into jail."

Kirk stood at the window looking out at Kate's back yard with its garden. She had already begun to spade it. Kate had a way of making things grow. He knew how the garden would look in another month or two, weedless and with long rows of lush vegetables.

"You listening to me, Kirk?"

He turned from the window. "I'm listening, but I don't see that what you've said has changed anything."

"Can't you see what that did to him?" she demanded. "He throwed away ten years of hard work and didn't have a dime to show for it, so he gritted his teeth and came to Colorado, swearing he'd make it on his own. He'd save and scrimp and he wouldn't give nothing to nobody. I'm not saying it was right, mind, and it sure as hell was hard on your ma. Likely that's why she's dead."

She heaved a long sigh. "He's bound to hate himself for a while. That's why he'll need you."

Kirk was silent, and Kate said, "There's something else it won't hurt you any to think on. You leave again and Guy'll

30

be so damned mad he'll fix it so you won't get an acre of Tomahawk. Matt and Billy will get it and they'll lose it. Want that to happen?"

"No." He reached into his vest pocket for tobacco and papers and deliberately rolled a smoke. Then he asked wearily, "All right, what do you want me to do?"

"That's better," she said. "I'm just asking you to stay in the country. Don't go away like you did before. I've got a hunch about this drought. Guy's going to have trouble, being the only cowman in the country who's got a surplus of grass."

Kirk nodded. "He'll have trouble, all right. He's already refused a deal with the Salt Creek bunch."

She sighed. "That's like him. How about it, Kirk? Will you stay?"

"I'll go back to Salt Creek," he said. "That way I'll be around if Matt or Billy needs me."

"Good." She took his hand and pumped it as a man would have. "It's settled, then."

"All right, Kate."

He went out through her plainly furnished parlor and into the wind which had turned cold again. Overhead, thin clouds had partially obscured the sun.

Kirk mounted and called to Kate in the doorway, "I'll get a rig and pick you up."

He headed toward O'Mara's saloon, thinking about Kate as he rode. She was nosey and bossy, and sometimes too much of a know-it-all, but she was all heart. It would serve Guy right if she married him. The old man would change pretty quick or he'd have his hands full.

And there was, he admitted reluctantly, something in what she'd said about understanding Guy. Knowing his father's background didn't make Kirk like him any better, but it helped him understand why Guy had been such a penny pincher all these years. Funny he'd never heard the story before. But not so funny, either, when he thought about it. Guy had never been a man to talk about himself.

Kirk's thoughts turned back to Tomahawk and he knew how it would be without his mother. His face turned somber. Depression and a sense of loss weighed heavily upon him. He decided he needed a drink.

Five

For reasons best known to the founders of the town, Jubilee was built around an open square in the fashion of the Spanish towns of the Southwest. But the center of this square held no bandstand, no monuments. Instead it contained a windmill, whirling crazily in the cold wind, and a stone watering trough.

Kirk angled across the square, heading toward O'Mara's saloon on the far corner. His horse splashed through the puddle that surrounded the watering trough, and put his muzzle down to drink. Kirk waited until he was through, eyeing O'Mara's place and the horses racked before it. He recognized Matt's bay, and another animal which carried the 3Y brand. It was the horse Shorty Hough had been riding yesterday.

Shorty must have ridden to town after the talk at the cow camp. Kirk lifted his horse's head from the trough and reined around, uneasiness stirring in him. But there was expectation, too. Shorty had been spoiling for a fight yesterday, and probably still was. If he wanted it bad enough, Kirk would accommodate him.

Crossing the square, Kirk dismounted in front of O'Mara's. He tied his horse, then climbed the three worn steps to the saloon door. The instant he entered he saw that something was wrong. Matt stood at the bar, a bottle and glass before him. His face was the brick red of a frustrated and embarrassed man, his eyes bloodshot from too many drinks. He was glaring at Shorty who lounged, laughing softly, at the end of the bar.

Kirk walked across the sawdust-covered floor to stand beside Matt. He said, "Hello, Matt."

Matt shoved the bottle at him. O'Mara slid a glass across the cherrywood bar. Kirk poured it a third full, raised it, and drained it, his gaze fixed steadily on Shorty.

The 3Y man's grin was cocky and dangerous, the grin of a man who was prodding trouble with a stick. He said, "If it ain't the other gold-plated son of the country's biggest bastard. The old man know you're drinkin', sonny?"

Kirk felt his muscles bunch and tighten. Shorty went on, "If he don't, he sure as hell will. Matt didn't have a thin dime in his jeans. He had to put the drinks on Tomahawk's bill."

A little core of red fury grew in Kirk's brain. He said, "I might ask you the same question, Shorty. Does Eli know you're in town doing your best to spoil his chance of getting grass from Tomahawk?"

Shorty laughed derisively. "What chance? Tomahawk ain't gonna let us have a blade of grass and you know it. Eli went to the wrong damned man. He should've seen Guy in the first place. You two don't have no more to say about how Tomahawk's run than the boy who drives the stacker team when you're hayin'."

Kirk's anger was lifting. Nerves tightened all over his body. He shared Matt's humiliation, suddenly, because what Shorty had said was true.

Shorty was hungering for a fight just as Kirk had known he would be, and Kirk felt an almost uncontrollable desire to oblige him, yet he held back. His mother lay dead out at Tomahawk, and in the circumstances he didn't want to roll around on the floor in a saloon brawl.

Shorty could have walked out with a moral victory, but there was a core of meanness, of vengefulness and jealousy in him that could not be satisfied with this. Possessed of an ugly face and a squat, unattractive body, he was uncertain of himself when it came to women. For a time Rachel Yockey had dispelled that uncertainty, but she had turned to Kirk when he'd bought the K Bar, a display of feminine fickleness that had fanned into a blaze the fury of jealousy which was in him.

He laughed mockingly. "I'll give some advice, sonny. Don't come back to that greasy-sack spread of yours. Nobody on Salt Creek wants a Van Horn for a neighbor. Eli or Luke Bartram or nobody. Bad enough to have 'em on top. And don't count on Rachel helpin' out none. Sooner or later she's goin' to see just how no-account you are." He turned his head to spit in the direction of the spittoon. "Anybody with a lick of sense'd know she was using you for what she could get, and by this time she likely knows there ain't nothing to use."

Matt said something under his breath and started toward

33

Shorty, but Kirk caught him by the arm and pulled him back.

Shorty laughed again. "Hell, I'll tell Eli to quit worryin'! Tomahawk's long on grass but short on guts. Guy's as bad as you are, yellow clean down to his backbone—if he's got one. I reckon we'll just move in and take what grass we need."

Kirk pushed himself away from the bar, prodded beyond endurance. "You're bound to have it, aren't you, Shorty? All right. Let's get it over with."

Shorty's grin died on his thick lips. His eyes were wicked with anticipation. He went into a crouch, weaving back and forth, as light on his feet as a cougar.

Suddenly Kirk noticed something about Shorty that he hadn't caught before. Shorty's nose was broken and flattened. His eyebrows were thick with scar tissue and his right ear was cauliflowered.

The 3Y man's ring-wise motion had made Kirk notice something he probably wouldn't have otherwise. It looked as if Shorty was an old hand at fighting, probably an ex-prize fighter who knew every trick in the book.

Kirk waited, standing straight, his hands at his sides. Shorty advanced, weaving, dancing lightly on the balls of his spurred and booted feet. He circled, and Kirk kept turning to face him, ready and tense as a starving wolf trying to kill for food. He was wholly unconscious of the other occupants of the saloon, who were watching with hungry anticipation, all of them aware of the deeper implications of this fight.

Shorty feinted, then threw a right. Kirk arched his body to one side, remaining upright, and the savage blow glanced off his ribs. Clasping his partly-raised hands, he brought them down with brutal force upon Shorty's neck.

Shorty stumbled and fell on his face, skidding in the sawdust for a foot before he stopped. He heaved himself up, brushing dust out of his eyes, shaking his head and wheezing. He glared at Kirk, cursing, then came on with a rush. Kirk was ready for him but he knew this time wouldn't be so easy. He'd have to take a lot of punishment before he could put Shorty down again.

He was right. He missed with a swing, and Shorty countered with a left that jarred and hurt and drove Kirk back on his heels. Shorty kept boring in, a little too eager, and

Kirk got a hard right past his guard that smashed him on the jaw. Shorty went down again, rolled over and jumped up, grunting with surprise.

He rushed again, but this time he never reached Kirk. A little man had stepped in through the door and without hesitation, crossed the room and stuck out a booted foot that tripped Shorty and sent him to the sawdust again.

Kirk turned angrily. "Stay out of it, Red."

The sheriff, Red Henessy, grinned. He was freckle-faced and scrawny, weighing little if any over a hundred and twenty pounds. But he was a fighter who never let his banty size keep him from tackling a bigger man.

"I'm already in, Kirk," Henessy said. "Now get on back to the bar and finish your drink."

Shorty got up, glaring at the tarnished star on Henessy's vest. "What the hell's the big idea . . ."

"Finish your drink peaceable or go to jail, Shorty," Henessy said. "Take your pick."

"So they own you, too." Shorty's voice was a shout of outrage. "How much you gettin', Red? Is it enough to pay for all the boot-lickin' you got to do?"

Henessy's expression didn't change except for the wicked, dancing light that came into his eyes. "You're all worked up, Shorty. We'll pretend you didn't say that. Just don't repeat it." His voice was deadly.

Shorty, knowing the sheriff, grumbled something under his breath as he brushed the sawdust from his clothes. He looked at Kirk, hatred a bright flame in his eyes. Then he whirled and tramped angrily from the saloon, slamming the door savagely behind him.

Henessy crossed to the bar as though nothing had happened. "Rye, O'Mara. Rye and water." His protruding Adam's apple bobbed in his skinny neck as he downed the drink.

Kirk returned to stand beside Matt and poured himself another drink. His hand was steady, but his belly felt as cold as if he had swallowed a full glass of ice water. What Shorty Hough had said about not being welcomed back on Salt Creek was probably true. Kirk dismissed what he had said about Rachel as the rantings of a jealous man, but no matter how much she wanted him to stay, she'd be helpless against

35

the tide of resentment that would flow against him simply because he was Guy Van Horn's son.

There was something else, too. He couldn't forget the last expression he'd seen on Shorty Hough's face, wild, almost crazy—a threat of mortal danger if he'd ever seen one.

Six

They buried Tessie Van Horn on the ridge above the Tomahawk buildings. Three other graves were there: those of an old roustabout who had died of typhoid when Kirk was a boy, a cow hand who had been thrown trying to break a bad horse, and another one who had been shot by rustlers when Guy had led his crew into the rough country west of Cathedral Rim after a band of stolen horses.

Standing beside the open grave, Kirk thought that this was no fit place to bury his mother. The cemetery in town would have been better. She'd been lonely all her life and had found comfort only in her sons and in Kate Gorman when Kate came for her summer visits. Kirk was sure she'd found no comfort in Guy. Now, in death, her loneliness would continue.

Matt stood on one side of Kirk, young Billy on the other. Billy was crying unashamedly. Matt's eyes were wet, but there were no tears in Kirk's. He listened with only half an ear to the singing of the old familiar hymns.

All the Tomahawk crew was here. Several people from town. Bianca and Delfino Chavez. Some ranchers and their families from north of White River. But no one from Salt Creek. Kirk wondered if they hadn't heard, or if they just didn't care, one way or the other.

He looked at Guy, who stood beside Kate. Guy's face was hard and cold, his mouth bitter and uncompromising. Kirk couldn't tell what his father was thinking or feeling—if he was feeling anything. And yet, studying him, Kirk thought he saw a dull pain in his father's eyes.

Kirk looked away from him and his eyes went again to Matt and Billy. It was his two brothers who were hurt the

36

most, who would miss their mother most; she'd been a buffer between them and their father, helping all she could. No doubt Kate was right. He had to stay in the country, even though he would have preferred to put it far behind him, to ride away from his little outfit on Salt Creek, leaving it for Eli Yockey or Luke Bartram or any of his neighbors who wanted it. And then there was Rachel. . . .

He shook his head, bringing his mind back to the present. The preacher read from the Bible, then he talked about the beautiful mansion that waited in heaven for Tessie Van Horn, the gold-paved streets and the perfect joy that would be hers while she sat at the side of her Master.

Words, Kirk thought rebelliously. Empty words. His mother had wanted no mansion and no streets of gold. His mother had only wanted to work, to be a mother to her sons, a wife to her husband. Why couldn't God have worked things out better—given her a little more while she was here—a little less now that she was gone? Kirk knew the preacher wouldn't understand his thoughts. He'd probably call him sacrilegious. But neither would the preacher have understood Tessie Van Horn, or the things that had made her what she was.

The preacher made a too-long prayer, while everyone stood shivering, heads bared to the stiff, cold wind. Still Kirk only half listened, his thoughts turning to Kate, who had taken charge from the moment Kirk pulled the livery stable rig to a stop in front of the house and carried her two heavy valises into the front room. He'd wondered then why she had brought two valises just to stay for a night or two, and he still didn't know.

He thought about how Kate had glanced around the long room, and then had looked at Guy. "Good Lord, man, how long are you going to keep using this room to store your plagued supplies?" For once Guy had held his tongue.

Kate had helped Bianca dress Kirk's mother in her one good satin dress. She had lined the coffin with white cloth she had brought from town. Bianca had gone home then, and Kate had cooked supper and sat up all night with the body. She was made of iron, Kirk thought. She was the kind of woman Guy should have married. Yet Kirk was glad his mother had been who she was.

The prayer was over at last. A final hymn. Still Kirk stood with his head bowed, the sound a distant one to his ears. He was thinking of obligations, and of the things that gave them birth. Perhaps Kate had been thinking of much the same thing when she'd talked of loyalty to Tomahawk.

Kirk couldn't agree with Kate that he owed anything to Guy Van Horn. He had made it plain to her that morning that he couldn't forget and forgive all at once. The old wounds were too deep. There was no real friendliness between him and Guy, not now anyway. Maybe there would be later after time had done its healing. Kate's advice that he stick with his family and watch out for the Salt Creek bunch was good, but it wasn't advice he could take now. Perhaps, back of everything else, was his desire to show Guy he could make good on his own.

Regardless of his feelings toward his father, Kirk did not question Kate's statement that he owed loyalty to Matt and Billy, to his mother's memory, to Tomahawk. And loyalty and obligation were inseparable. Matt and Billy needed help to escape the vise that Kirk had escaped five years ago, else they'd never become the men their mother had so desperately wanted them to be. . . .

The service was over. The preacher closed his Bible and stepped back. Some of the men picked up shovels and began to fill the grave.

There were no flowers this time of year, nothing but the paper roses Kate had brought from town. Kirk turned away, his arm over Billy's shoulder. His mother should have had flowers, at least. Yes, she should have had flowers. . . .

Walking down the slope toward the house with the cold spring wind knifing at them from the valley; Billy wiped his shirt sleeve across his face. He swallowed and looked around at the somber crowd. This was part of growing and becoming a man, this hiding of emotion, but Kirk said, "No shame in grieving, Billy."

"Ma always said tears never changed anything."

"And so they don't, but they relieve a man's feelings."

Billy looked his thanks at Kirk.

After that they walked in silence to the house, the others following. Kirk saw that Bianca and Delfino had gone on ahead. He didn't want to talk to anyone except Bianca and

Kate. He could see Kate before he left, and he could swing by the Chavez cabin on his way to Salt Creek.

Billy wandered off toward the barn and Kirk turned into the house, anxious to be gone. He went up to his room and quickly stuffed the few things he'd need into his canvas warsack. Then he slung it onto the bed, changed his clothes and buckled his gun and belt around his waist. He laid his Winchester beside the warsack and for a long time stood at the window, his back to it, thinking how his mother had kept his room without change for the five years he'd been gone.

She'd had a lot of faith. She'd known he'd be back. Now he wondered if he'd ever come back again. Not as long as his father was here, he told himself, and Guy Van Horn was indestructible.

He heard angry words from downstairs. Guy and Kate were quarreling. Anger stirred in him. Couldn't the old man forego fighting even on a day like this?

Impatiently he picked up his warsack and Winchester, went down the stairs and out through the back door. Neither Kate nor Guy, intent on each other, noticed him.

Guy stood on the porch shaking hands with the townspeople and ranchfolks who had come to the funeral. Doc Peters was the last to leave. As he took Guy's reluctantly offered hand, he said, "Guy, you think you're as tough as a boot heel or you wouldn't push yourself the way you do. Ease up or you'll be where your wife is."

Guy uttered a brief obscenity. "Mail me your bill," he said, "but keep your advice."

"The advice is free," Doc said caustically, "and you'd better listen to it. You work too hard and you've got too damned much temper. Control it or it'll be the death of you. Your blood pressure . . ."

"Is going up by the minute," Guy broke in. "I told you once before to get out of here. Now I'm telling you again."

He whirled away, controlling his anger with difficulty. It should be enough, having to pay the damned sawbones for coming out here from Jubilee, but he wasn't going to listen to and pay Doc for telling him something he already knew. He'd had high blood pressure for a long time and he was still alive and kicking.

He saw Matt by the barn and called, "Harness up that livery team. Kate'll be ready to go in a minute."

He stomped into the house, still swearing under his breath at the doctor. He found Kate standing in the middle of the cluttered living room. He said, "Matt's hooking up for you."

She didn't move, and when he looked at her broad, stubborn face, he saw she was going to give him trouble. He added grudgingly, "Thanks for comin' out."

"You're welcome." She looked him straight in the eyes. "I'm not going back to town. You need a woman here. So do the boys. I'm staying."

"We don't need no woman," Guy said harshly. "Go on back where you belong."

She looked at him pityingly. "You still don't know how much Tessie did, do you? Who's going to cook and wash for you? You going to do it for yourself?" She threw out a hand in a gesture of exasperation. "Look at this room—a damned storehouse because you're too stingy to build one. You don't have a single place in the house where a body can sit down and rest. I heard what Doc said. Now go on and blow up if you've got to, but do it before Doc gets out of the yard."

He shouted, "You ain't, by God, staying here! So get out before I carry you out."

A grin stirred the corners of her wide mouth. "Now that'll be something to see. Come on, Guy, carry me out."

Guy was speechless with fury. Damn her! Damn this woman anyway!

Still grinning, she said, "So that's settled. I'm staying, though I wonder, really, why I bother with you." Her eyes were sharp and seemed to look right through him. "Maybe you're worried about how much I'll eat and how much you'll have to pay me. Well, damn your soul, I'll eat all I please, which is going to be considerable, and you won't pay me anything. I'll cook and clean house and wash your dirty clothes and patch 'em." She waggled a stubby forefinger at him. "You run the outfit, but everything within a hundred yards of the house is woman's work—my work. Savvy?"

"Get out! Damn it, get out, I said!"

She was taunting him. "All right, carry me out. There's still a few folks in the yard to see you do it."

He roared, "All right! All right! Stay and be damned."

40

"I'll stay, all right. You need somebody and you know it. You've purely made a mess of things. You ran Kirk off when he was eighteen. You broke Matt till he's only half a man, and you'll do the same with Billy if somebody doesn't stop you. Well, I aim to stop you. And another thing. You're chasing Kirk right into the middle of that scheming Salt Creek bunch, and you know they'll make life hell for him if you don't give them the grass they want."

He stood ten feet from her, his blood pounding crazily in his temples, rage pouring through his body, and all the time he really respected her because she was one person who had never been afraid of him and never would. He wheeled to the door and stalked out.

Kate called after him, "Supper's at six."

He slammed the front door, yelling at Matt, "Put that team away. You'll have to take 'em to town in the morning. Kate's staying."

He strode across the yard to where Kirk was tightening the cinch. He noted the warsack tied behind the saddle. He said, "You can't pull out now. There's work to do here."

Kirk stepped into the saddle, his head tipped forward, eyes on his father. He said, "I wouldn't have worked during roundup if Ma hadn't asked me to. No reason to stay now."

"No reason?" Guy bellowed. "This is your home, ain't it?"

"Not any more. My home's on Salt Creek."

Again blood pulsed in Guy's forehead. "You go now, you don't come back! Starve to death on your hardscrabble range if you want to, but don't ask me for help. And don't look for a share of Tomahawk. You won't get it."

Kirk gave him a steady look and rode away, his mouth a bitter line. Guy stared after him. He hadn't meant what he'd said. He hadn't meant it at all. He wanted to shout at Kirk to come back, wanted to tell him he hadn't meant anything he said, but he couldn't make himself do it.

The enormity of his loss suddenly hit him. First Tessie. Now Kirk. He didn't feel the chill April wind. For the first time in years he was whipped, and all his wealth and power couldn't change that fact.

Seven

A feeling of finality oppressed Kirk as he rode away from Tomahawk. This was not at all like the time he had left five years ago. Then there had been a note of excitement in it, of adventure. His mother had stood on the front porch waving to him, and he'd known that someday he'd return.

No, this was different. Oh, he'd see Guy occasionally just as he'd see his brothers. You couldn't live in the same country without seeing other people who lived there, too, but that wasn't the same as living with them.

He crossed the vast meadows and left them, and took to the timber heading west. Presently he reined up before the Chavez cabin. He had intended only to say good-bye, but when Bianca opened the door and called, "Kirk, come on in," he changed his mind. He swung down, leaving the reins dragging, and went in.

Delfino wasn't in sight. As Bianca shut the door, Kirk asked, "Where's Delfino?"

"Gone." She walked to the stove and stirred up the fire. "Sit down, Kirk. I'll have coffee for you in a minute."

He was always surprised when he came here; there was so much difference between the Chavez cabin and the huge, gloomy house on Tomahawk or his shack on Salt Creek. This room was light and pleasant.

There was a shining look about the place. Starched gingham curtains hung at the windows. Bright-colored rag rugs were on the well-scrubbed floor. The room had a warm, lived-in look. Delfino's newspaper, a week-old Jubilee *Chronicle*, lay on the floor beside his rocker. There was a half-smoked pipe in the ash tray. A pair of worn sheepskin slippers had been set on a footstool in front of the chair.

The loneliness which was always present in his cabin on the K Bar and the friction which he invariably felt when he was in the Tomahawk ranch house were not here. Was it just Bianca's presence? Or was it a natural touch she had for housekeeping? Or both? He didn't know. He only knew he hated to leave.

"Delfino didn't waste much time," Kirk said.

"He thought a lot of your mother. The funeral was almost more than he could stand." She smiled gently. "He wasn't made to live inside four walls. He thinks better, off by himself."

Kirk said, "I'm leaving Tomahawk, Bee. I'm going back to the K Bar. Tell Delfino to drop in on me when he can."

"I'll tell him."

She was watching him intently. It made him self-conscious. He rolled a cigarette, his gaze dropping to the oil cloth that covered the table. Bianca got the coffee from the stove and poured it, her boot heels pounding hard on the cabin floor. She returned the pot to the stove, then came back and sat down across from him.

She traced the design on the oil cloth with her finger tip, her eyes following the finger. "I despise your father, Kirk. I can't help it. I've seen what he's done to you and your brothers. I know you can't stay." She glanced up, smiling. "But I wish you could."

He drank his coffee. The storm that had been gathering in him all day faded into serenity. He studied the girl until her gaze dropped. At times she was violent of temper. She was always strong and active, always direct. Yet, at moments like this, there was softness and gentleness in her, too.

If he never saw her again, his memories of her would be . . .

He smiled, thinking of her as she'd been before he went away five years ago, riding bareback like an Indian, braids flying, bare legs shining in the sun. He remembered her fighting with Matt, and coming out of it with her nose skinned and her hair streaming loosely around her pixie face. But he'd remember her the way she was today, too.

Then he thought of Rachel Yockey. He'd come close to asking Rachel to marry him, but he wasn't sure he loved her, not the way a man should love a wife. She had a way of building a fire in him whenever he was with her. He had little doubt he could possess her, for instinct told him that was the kind of woman she was. He wanted her, all right, but marrying her was something else. Perhaps he felt this

43

reluctance now because he was with Bianca—but he'd been more like a brother to Bianca than anything else, and no doubt that was the way she thought of him . . . or did she?

Bianca put her hands palm down on the table and leaned toward Kirk. "What are you going to do if your father keeps on refusing to share his range?"

He said, "I've only got twenty-five head of cattle. They'll . . ."

"I mean about the others. What will they do?"

"I don't know. Shorty's already threatened to take range away from Tomahawk."

"He wouldn't really try, would he? Eli wouldn't let him."

"Eli's getting old. Sometimes I wonder whether Eli or Shorty runs the 3Y. I think it depends on how much backing he gets from Luke Bartram and Chet Tappan and the rest."

"Then where will you stand? When the chips are down, you'll find you're more loyal to your father than you think."

Her words disturbed him. He didn't know if she was right or not, but he said, "I'll never come back just because he needs me."

"What about Matt and Billy?" she demanded. "Where will you stand if it comes to a fight? You can't fight Tomahawk and you can't stay neutral. That bunch on Salt Creek won't let you."

"Maybe Guy will change his mind."

"He'll never change," she said bitterly. "You know that."

He rose and stood looking down at her, feeling a sudden unbidden desire to take her into his arms. As he picked up his hat, he thought that if it had been Rachel he probably would have grabbed her and drawn her, compliant, into a passionate embrace.

"I've got to go," he said. "I'll have to stop at Hank Pike's store on the way home if I'm going to eat tonight."

She followed him outside, watching as he stepped into the saddle. He gave her a wry grin. "I'll see you one of these days." He rode away, and crossing the meadow, disappeared into the brush and timber on the far side.

She watched until he was gone, a storm building in her like clouds piling up over Cathedral Rim in midsummer. Then she whirled and ran into the cabin.

The storm broke in her and she kicked a chair. She'd

44

tried to tell Kirk the things he needed to know about himself, but she'd botched it. Kate had told her to let him know she had faith in him.

"He's a lost soul," Kate had said. "He's been fighting Guy and himself and everything else until he just don't know which way to turn. He needs someone to hang onto. Let him hang onto you, Bee."

She'd tried and failed, and the fault was hers. For the first time he had appeared to realize she was more than a girl, that he had a need for her, but when he'd got that look in his eyes she had let her own face go stiff and inexpressive. She didn't know why, for she had wished that he'd reach out to her. Perversely she had killed the very impulse she had tried to encourage. There was no explanation of her failure, none whatever.

At that moment she hated herself. She remembered telling Delfino that she would do more than ride double with Kirk if she had to, but instead, she had discouraged the first hint of an advance he had ever made.

She sat down at the table and put her head into her arms. She began to cry.

Kirk rode up country and topped the plateau, then took the winding trail down off Cathedral Rim into Salt Creek. He kept thinking about the questions Bianca had raised, but he was certain only about one thing. He had done the right thing in leaving, for staying would only have meant a quarrel with Guy so bitter they could never make up.

Now he had to decide where he would stand if the grazing question came to a fight. He honestly didn't know. Not yet.

Kirk reached Salt Creek in late afternoon and reining up in front of the store, dismounted. There was no real settlement here, just a weather-beaten log building that was the store, and a schoolhouse across the road.

The creek was the lowest he had ever seen it. Usually at this time of year the runoff of melting snow was beginning to swell it, but there would be no runoff this year because there was no snow.

Eli Yockey and Luke Bartram and the others that Kirk knew had their ranches on Salt Creek. Bigger outfits had prior rights to the water. With no more water in the creek than this, it was certain that the big ranches would take all of it. Eli and his neighbors wouldn't make a single stack of hay on their burned-out fields. Neither would Kirk.

Without new grass on Buck Point, they'd be faced with no alternative but to sell the herds which had taken them years to build up, and at giveaway prices since the animals would be thin. Kirk would be wiped out, too, but his would be a small loss compared to the others'.

If there was no graze anywhere in the country, the Salt Creekers might take their impending ruin philosophically in the way of cattlemen from time immemorial. But there was grass in the country—grass not needed and going to waste, grass for which their offer of a reasonable rental had been contemptuously refused.

They'd look across the fence that cut Buck Point off from the rest of the plateau; they'd see the grass that Tomahawk didn't need, and they'd listen to Shorty Hough's inflammatory words, and then there'd be trouble—shooting trouble such as Tomahawk hadn't faced for years. It wouldn't be helped by the fact that the Salt Creek people had originally run their cattle all over the plateau and had been pushed by Guy Van Horn onto Buck Point by force.

But it was out of Kirk's hands now. He went into the store, troubled and uneasy. Hank Pike, standing behind the counter, was as dried up as a last year's cottonwood leaf, a small man who had ridden for Tomahawk years ago. He'd broken horses for Guy, but when he'd become too crippled up from forking the rough ones to work any more, Guy had simply let him go. As a result, Pike nursed a savage hatred for Guy and for Tomahawk.

When Kirk came in, Pike said grudgingly, "Sorry about your ma, Kirk. She was the one good thing about Tomahawk."

Kirk said, "Thanks, Hank. I need some grub."

Pike wrote Kirk's order on a piece of paper, then he looked up. "What you going to do down here?"

"Ranch. What else?"

"With twenty-five head? Are you crazy?"

"Other men have started with less."

"Not in years like this." Pike stared at him suspiciously. "Wouldn't be that Guy sent you down here, would it?

46

Wouldn't be he wants to know what the Salt Creek boys are thinking, would it?"

"You trying to say I'd spy on my own neighbors?"

"You catch on quick. 'Course you won't have no trouble with your twenty-five head. You'll just turn 'em in on Tomahawk."

Kirk shook his head wearily. There was no reason why he had to explain himself to Hank Pike. But he said, "Guy wouldn't give me any grass. We had a row."

"Sure, you had a row," Pike said. "Try telling that to Shorty. Or Luke."

Kirk felt his anger rise. "You going to get that grub or not, Pike?"

"I'll get it, but it's my guess you won't be around long enough to eat it."

Pike started to put together the things on Kirk's list. Kirk waited, thinking sourly he couldn't blame Pike for his suspicions. But it was going to make living down here damned hard. He had to work with these people. A man didn't run cattle in the Salt Creek breaks alone. He couldn't.

Right now Kirk's twenty-five head were scattered from one end of Salt Creek to the other, a distance of nearly forty miles. He wouldn't find them by himself if he worked at it all summer. He needed the others. And he'd hoped they'd need and accept him.

Pike put his supplies in a box. Kirk carried it outside in time to see Rachel Yockey and Eli ride up with Luke Bartram. He put the box down and waited, wondering if his reception at Eli's hands would be any warmer than at Pike's. Bartram, a dark, barren-faced man who was Eli's neighbor to the north, stood waiting to see what he did.

Eli nodded at Kirk briefly, his eyes cold and unfriendly. Kirk turned to Rachel. Her face was troubled, so he knew they had talked to Shorty Hough.

He said to Eli, "Guy refused the grass. Maybe if you went to him . . ."

"I wouldn't ask Guy Van Horn for a drink if I was dyin' of thirst!"

"I'm sorry," Kirk said. "I even broke with him over it. I've come back here to live."

47

"I don't give a damn what you do," Eli growled, and stomped into the store, Bartram following.

Kirk felt Rachel's hand on his arm. "This isn't going to be easy for you, Kirk. They don't trust you because you're a Van Horn and right now they're blaming all their troubles on the Van Horns."

He said, "And Shorty's making it hotter by building a fire under 'em."

She nodded. "You'll have to prove you're one of them. Can you do that, Kirk?"

He didn't know. Rachel certainly didn't seem worried. Instead, he thought he detected something that looked like satisfaction in her eyes—as though she had seen in him the answers she wished to see to the question she'd asked.

Her hand tightened intimately on his arm. "I missed you at the dance. If I'd known about your mother . . ."

"There'll be other dances," he said.

Suddenly he wanted to take her into his arms, and he remembered thinking that she would never have stayed remote the way Bianca had. Her lips parted slightly, her breasts rose and fell with her hastened breathing. Her eyes gave him an unmistakable promise but as he started to reach for her he heard Eli's boot-heels and the ring of his spurs as he crossed the porch.

Kirk looked at Eli, conscious of the heightened color in his face. He asked, "When you starting spring roundup, Eli?"

"We've already started." Eli's eyes were still unfriendly. "If you want to work with us, be at my place at sunup."

Eli balanced the box he carried on his saddle horn, settling it before him. Rachel gave Kirk a final squeeze on his arm and mounted. They rode away, Rachel looking back over her shoulder at him.

There was a lot of woman. . . .

Eight

Kirk's K Bar lay upstream from Eli Yockey's 3Y about a mile. He had bought it six months before, shortly after he had returned, using the money he'd saved during the five years he'd been away. He owned 160 acres of bottom land, of which about half was in hay and under the ditch. The buildings were inadequate, a one-room log cabin chinked with adobe mud and roofed with sod, and a tottering shed made of rough-sawed lumber.

Still, it was with some pride that Kirk surveyed the ranch from the road as he opened the gate and went through. This was the first land he had ever owned; it was his to do with as he saw fit, and it gave him a sense of satisfaction he had never felt before in his life.

Guy had scoffed at the place, and at Kirk for buying it, yet it was more than Guy had started with so many years before. Perhaps Kirk would never build it into the empire Tomahawk was. But he could build it into a home and a comfortable one. One thing was sure. He wouldn't make the mistake Guy had. He wouldn't alienate family and neighbors because he was forever greedy for more.

He dismounted in the gray of dusk and led his horse into the shed. He unsaddled and put the animal into the single stall, then he went outside and forked hay from the four-foot-high butt of his single haystack through the window of the shed. This done, he went into the cabin and lighted the coal-oil lamp.

The cabin was less tight and less comfortable than one of Tomahawk's cow camps, but the comparison did not occur to Kirk. He built up the fire, then went to the creek for a bucket of water. He carried in his box of supplies, and while the stove heated he swept the packed dirt floor of the cabin.

Outside on one of the cedar-covered benches, a coyote lifted his voice at the rising moon. Kirk heard his horse stirring in the shed out back of the cabin.

He cooked his supper, and ate it, and afterward turned in immediately. It had been a long day, filled with tension and strain. If he was any judge, tomorrow would be even worse. Shorty Hough, and perhaps Eli and Luke Bartram, too, would have the Salt Creek ranchers stirred up until they were openly hostile to him.

He'd have to take it, he thought as he stared upward toward the black ceiling. He'd have to take it if he was ever going to carve a place for himself here on Salt Creek.

He went to sleep with the soft rush of the creek in his ears, the sounds of night animals moving about outside his cabin. He was up and riding while the morning was still dark. He reached the 3Y as dawn began to streak the high-piled pinnacles of Cathedral Rim to the east.

Eli's place rested tight and snug in a grove of monstrous cottonwoods. Like most of the other houses hereabouts, it was constructed of logs, but unlike Kirk's small cabin, it was not chinked with mud but with concrete. It had a gabled roof with great, wide eaves which gave it a homey, permanent look.

Horses were tied at various places in the yard, fifteen or twenty in all. These were the mounts of the Salt Creek ranchers who would ride today rounding up the cattle from the cedar hills and from the breaks high under the rim.

Kirk paused on the porch to wash, then went to the kitchen door and knocked. There was so much noise of talking inside the kitchen that he wasn't heard, so he opened the door and went in. The air was rich with the smell of cooking food. Men were seated on both sides of a great, long table, and Rachel and Marge Yockey, Eli's young, second wife, were serving.

Rachel glanced up as he came in, a smile lighting her face. She brushed a wisp of hair away from her damp forehead with the back of her hand. She was tall for a girl, but still several inches short of Kirk's six feet. Today she wore a dress with an extremely tight bodice and waist so that her breasts showed proud and plain beneath it. The skirt flared below the waist, but not before it had revealed the swell of her rounded hips.

It occurred to Kirk that Rachel had worn this dress because she knew he would be here, and it had the desired effect on him. She always had a way of exciting him, but more than usual this morning; his thoughts would be turning to her all day.

She put down the coffee pot she was carrying and crossed the kitchen to him. Her smile said she had been waiting for him and him alone. "Hello, Kirk. I've saved you a place right here beside Pa. Come and sit down."

He sailed his hat into the corner and sat down beside Eli. Shorty was seated directly across the table from him.

Preoccupied with Rachel, Kirk had not noticed how the conversation died as he came in. Now he could not fail to notice it, for the room was coldly still.

"Well, look who's here," Shorty said, his voice clear and plain. "Now we can get somethin' done, boys. The expert's on the job."

Eli glanced at Rachel, hesitated, and then said, "Shut up, Shorty."

"Sure, Eli. Sure I'll shut up. I don't want everything I say carried back to Guy Van Horn."

There was a murmur along the table at that. Luke Bartram nodded and said, "That's sure as hell right."

Kirk clenched his hands beneath the edge of the table. Rachel served him over his left shoulder, brushing so close that her hair tickled his cheek. Shorty's face turned red.

Kirk met Shorty's stare steadily, feeling his own anger begin to burn. There was no excuse for this. Shorty was going to make it as tough as he could. He was still convinced he could beat Kirk half to death with his fists and was aching for an opportunity to try.

"You've tangled with me once, Shorty," Kirk said, "but we never got it finished. Next time we will. It'll be a pleasure to show you up for a fourflusher. You bet and I'll call."

A growl ran the length of the table. Kirk, glancing along the line of faces, found their stares as unfriendly as Shorty's. He said, "Boys, from now on I live on Salt Creek. My cattle are running with yours. It's my right to ride on roundup with you. Anybody want to challenge that right?"

"Hold on now," Eli said in a peremptory tone. "Nobody says you can't ride with us. I invited you myself. Shorty, you keep your damn lip buttoned. There ain't a bit of grass left out in the cedars. We got to get our cattle gathered an' out on top. I'll be damned if we're goin' to be set back because you two fightin' cocks can't get along. You understand?"

Shorty shrugged, a faint smile lingering at the corners of his wide mouth. His expression was as belligerent as ever, but when his eyes dropped away from Kirk's, they made a promise. Kirk attacked his breakfast. He doubted if he could whip Shorty with his fists, but when the time came, he'd sure as hell let Shorty know he'd been in a fight.

He finished eating and rolled a cigarette with steady fingers.

51

Eli had been watching him and Shorty by turns, and now as he lighted his pipe, he said to Shorty, "We've only got three or four more days of roundup and then we'll be ready to go out on top. You catch yourself a pack string today and take grub and salt up on the mountain. By the time we're done, you'll have the cabin stocked and the summer's salt on top."

For a moment Kirk thought Shorty was going to defy Eli, but in the end he dropped his glance and shrugged. Eli rose from the table and went out, the others trooping behind him. Shorty hung back to talk to Rachel, so Kirk only smiled at her as he went out.

It was grueling work. The men split up after leaving the 3Y, one group taking the east side of the valley, the other the west. Three men rode along the valley floor with the cattle that had been gathered the day before.

Chet Tappan, in charge of the crew with which Kirk rode, put him at the hardest job, that of riding under the high spires of Cathedral Rim. He accepted the assignment without comment. In a way he was glad, for if he had been given the easiest job, it would have been indicative of Chet's contempt.

Kirk put his horse up the treacherous slide, making a trail as he went across, and finally reached the shelf that ran directly under the rim, small avalanches of shale marking his route across the slide.

In this position he was forced to ride twice as far as any of the others, and over rough, dangerous footing. He found cattle in the little brushy draws that fingered away from the foot of the rim, and each time when he had gathered enough, he drove them downslope to the next man on his right. Then he'd go back.

In this way the day passed, with no halt for dinner. Instead, the men worked steadily through the day; the only rest they had came when their horses were so heated and winded that they had to stop.

At night Kirk rode home and collapsed on his bunk, instantly dead to the world. In the morning he was up an hour before dawn and riding again.

They worked down the valley as the days progressed, the gather steadily increasing until on the fourth day Eli said,

"We'll send four men out to gather strays. The rest of us will start branding."

So they held the herd at a wide place in the valley while men rode through, dragging out calves one by one. Dust rose in a cloud. Calves bawled, and their terrified cries were answered by the outraged, indignant ones of the mothers. A cow followed each bawling calf, and the man with the iron read the cow's brand and slapped the same brand on the calf's quivering hip.

Six hundred cattle held in a single bunch. Three separate branding fires raising smoke to the sky. Fifteen or more sweating, cursing men working the daylight hours away.

Arguments broke out hourly, as each man tried jealously to watch the work of all three branders to see that no calves were mis-marked. You weren't casual about mistakes when you had as tight a time making it as these men did.

Out of Kirk's twenty-five cows, twenty-two were found. And he had eighteen clean, new whitefaced calves to wear the K Bar. It was exhilarating to realize that. This was his first increase, his first step toward real independence from Tomahawk.

Still, there was a crawling uneasiness in him for all of his exhilaration. He could never quite rid his mind of the question Bianca had asked. What would he do when the showdown came with Tomahawk?

And come it would. Grass was gone from the cedars and from under the rim. He knew there was little or no grass on Buck Point. These were obvious facts that all the Salt Creek ranchers knew as well as he did, yet they were proceeding exactly as though there was grass on Buck Point. They were making their customary roundup, and when it was over they'd make their customary drive up the trail and out on top.

Kirk realized there was nothing else they could do. But he also realized they were moving toward open war with Tomahawk. Blindly, perhaps, but the end was inevitable. He knew cowmen too well to think that any of them would watch their cattle starve and do nothing about it.

He wondered if, when Guy realized that the Salt Creek bunch had their cattle out on Buck Point, he would put a guard on the fence separating that range from Tomahawk. Probably he would. And then the trouble would begin.

A heavy rain or snow could save the situation, but except for that high, thin haze, the sky was without a cloud, and had been so for weeks. During the winter there had been scarcely a drop of moisture. Kirk had no reason to believe the situation would change now. Every sign pointed to a hot, dry summer.

The days passed; the backbreaking work of branding continued until all the calves were marked. The men who had been gathering strays came in, then one morning the bunch of them started the cattle toward the trail leading to the top.

They drove down Salt Creek to Dry Salt Wash, which separated Buck Point from the main plateau, came into it, then took the cattle up the wash as it lifted toward the rim. The cattle were weak and thin. Many of the older cows were lost that day. They lay down, spirit and will to live gone. Some tumbled off the shelf trail where it neared the top. With each one that died, the faces of the Salt Creek ranchers grew a little more grim.

Kirk thought, *You'd better give them grass, Guy. You'd better give them grass or men will die the way these cattle are dying.*

They topped the trail and came out on Buck Point. The cattle began to scatter, hunting for grass. They browsed the dry brush upon which there were no leaves. They bawled and stared reproachfully with dumb eyes at the men who had brought them here.

Kirk stared at the same men. And they met his stare with cold, hating ones of their own that said: *You're a Van Horn. You're not one of us. You could help us, but you won't.*

Premonition was a coldness along Kirk's spine. He knew he would never be one of these men until the question of range had been settled. At times he wondered if he would ever be one of them. Their conversation stilled whenever he came within earshot. They looked at him suspiciously, without trust. Not for one minute did they forget he was a Van Horn.

How would they proceed? And when? Would they wait a while, or would they cut Tomahawk fence at once? Would they count on the cattle to find the breaks in the fence, or would they throw caution to the winds and drive them through?

Kirk shook his head, unable to guess what these men would

54

do any more than he could predict how Guy would retaliate. Guy might simply drive their cattle back onto Buck Point and repair the fence, thereafter keeping it guarded. Or he might order the Salt Creek cattle shot wherever and whenever he found them. Kirk knew he was capable of it.

There were a few days before the trouble would erupt. During those days a miracle might come about. Perhaps Guy would relent.

The cow camp cabin of the Salt Creek bunch was a low log cabin with a flat sod roof. Kirk's muscles and nerves tightened as he approached it, for he was aware that his long overdue showdown with Shorty was near. Eli might keep Shorty in check for a few hours, but he couldn't hold him back for long.

Kirk knew that, win, lose or draw, the inevitable fight with Shorty would make his position even more precarious with his neighbors than it was now. So, when he reined up in front of the cabin and saw Rachel Yockey come through the door, he had an uneasy feeling that this was the showdown. Shorty waited behind her in the doorway, a big hand gripping the casing above his head. He scowled when he saw Kirk.

"Dinner's ready," Rachel called. "Wash up and come on in. You look thin, Kirk; you've been working too hard."

He said, "So's everybody else. But it's over now. The stuff's all branded and out on top."

He saw her brows draw together and worry creep into her usually serene face. "Is it over, Kirk? Or is it only beginning?"

"Maybe it'll rain. Don't borrow trouble."

She nodded and turned away, giving him an uncertain smile before she went back into the cabin. Kirk walked to the spring behind the cabin and washed in the icy stream that trickled from the pipe.

The others came in, by ones and twos, and all trooped into the cabin to eat, giving Rachel a hearty welcome: they liked her cooking better than Shorty's.

In the afternoon they packed salt out to various points on Buck Point to help scatter the cattle, and again that evening Rachel had a savory meal of venison and potatoes ready when they came in.

The sky grew dark with coming night. Kirk, sitting outside smoking a cigarette, was surprised when Rachel came silently

55

up behind him. "I've got to go, Kirk. There's no place for a woman around a cow camp at night. Will you ride with me a ways?"

He hesitated, thinking of Shorty, and then rebellion flared up in him. Why should he let thoughts of Shorty dictate his actions? He rose. "Wait till I saddle my horse."

He went to the log corral and roped out his horse. He saddled the animal and led him to the cabin where Rachel waited. In the darkness he couldn't see Shorty, but he sensed that the man was watching jealously from somewhere. To hell with him. Let him stew.

Rachel led out, and Kirk followed immediately behind. It was the warmest night they'd had so far. The sky was clear and the stars were very bright. Kirk kept listening for sounds of a horse behind them, thinking that Shorty might follow, but he heard nothing.

For a time they rode in silence, the only sounds the crackling of their horses' hoofs in the dry sagebrush. When they reached the place where the trail started down, Rachel suddenly reined her horse to a stop and dismounted.

Kirk pulled up, hesitated, then stepped down. Rachel, holding her horse's reins, sank to the ground. From here the land sloped sharply away to the rim, and the whole Salt Creek valley was visible, vast and deep, a well of inky blackness relieved only by the few flickering lights of the ranches along the creek. Off to their right a deer spooked away noisily. Somewhere a wolf howled, making Kirk think of Delfino and then of Bianca.

Rachel sighed, lying back. "It's a lovely night, Kirk. Or it would be if it weren't for all this trouble."

"It's a nice night, all right," he agreed.

"What are you going to do, Kirk?"

"I don't know," he said. "I've got to stand with your father and his friends, but I can't fight my own father and brothers, if it comes to a fight. Seems like I'm caught anyway I look at it."

"Promise me one thing, Kirk," she murmured.

"What?"

"Promise me you won't do anything foolish. After all, Guy is your father."

He looked down at her, resting on an elbow. Her face was

56

a soft blur in the starlight, but he could see that her lips were slightly parted. Her words, contrary to what he expected of her, disturbed him.

She stirred, turning toward him, her breasts rising and falling quickly. Suddenly she was in his arms. His mouth found hers, warm and sweet. His body forced hers back to the ground and her arms were tight around his neck.

She drew her mouth from his and said, "Kirk, when can we get married?"

He didn't answer for a moment, feeling trapped and uncomfortable, and for some inexplicable reason his thoughts turned briefly to Bianca. He sat up, silent for a time as he examined his emotions, aware of the tremendous pull Rachel had had for him ever since his return. But he still wasn't sure of his real feeling for her, and now her question bothered him. It was, after all, the man's privilege to do the asking, not the woman's.

He got up abruptly and helped her to her feet. He said, "You'd better get on down the trail."

She hesitated, perhaps sensing she had said the wrong thing at the wrong time, that she should have waited. She raised her face for his kiss, but now the fire was gone. He lifted her into her saddle and stood there as she rode down the trail.

He mounted and rode back to the cow camp, vaguely wishing that Rachel was a little more like Bianca, or Bianca was a little more like Rachel. The truth was no man liked a woman to be too forward, and there was no doubt in his mind that Rachel would do anything for a man if she wanted him for a husband.

He shook his head, his thoughts sour. Like one of Delfino's wolves, he had sensed a trap. The knowledge that he might have taken the bait if Rachel had not asked when they were getting married only added to his bitterness.

Nine

Kirk expected everyone to be asleep when he returned, but as he crested the rise and headed down the draw toward the cabin, he saw that its windows were glowing with light. Several men stood in front of the cabin in a tight group. One of them carried a lantern.

All seemed to be looking toward the small, log storehouse which was set near the cabin on its right side. Frowning, Kirk rode close until he could hear sounds issuing from the open door of the storehouse. From the racket Kirk thought someone had run amuck inside, and was methodically wrecking it.

Ripped oat sacks came plummeting out through the door. A case of canned goods followed and smashed on the ground. A five-gallon syrup tin came out next, and broke, and then the occupant of the storehouse came shambling out to lick at the spilled syrup. It was Eli, Kirk's pet brown bear. Kirk, close now, began to chuckle.

Shorty Hough came boiling out of the cabin, a coiled rope in his hand. Kirk heard his enraged words, "Don't nobody shoot! I'm goin' to rope him and tie him up and then I'm goin' to beat the hell out of him with a quirt."

Kirk's grin widened. He reined up just outside the circle of lantern light and watched. This ought to be something to see. Time enough later to intervene if the bear got the worst of it, but Kirk didn't think he would.

The night horses in the corral were going wild, for the wind was blowing the terrifying bear scent toward them. They raced around the corral, rearing, bucking, snorting with fear.

Shorty advanced slowly, shaking out his loop. It sailed out as the bear raised his head warily to eye Shorty. The rope settled neatly over his head and tightened as Shorty laid back against it.

Eli growled softly. He pawed at the tightening rope, a ludicrous expression on his face. Kirk supposed that the bear was remembering the chain which had been around his neck all his life until he'd been turned loose. Suddenly he whirled around, dropped to all fours and shambled away.

Shorty had made the mistake of allowing slack to come into the rope. When the bear hit the end of it, he yanked Shorty off his feet, and went plunging out into the darkness. He crashed through the brush and timber, dragging Shorty along at the end of the rope.

Kirk began to laugh. Shorty disappeared. Luke Bartram

yelled, "Hang on, Shorty!" And Chet Tappan: "Hold him till I bring your quirt, Shorty!" The other men roared with mirth.

Kirk rode to the corral and put his horse inside. Then he walked back. The laughter was stilled now as everyone surveyed the damage, then one by one they turned to Kirk, their eyes accusing and hostile.

The damage was considerable. Oats and shredded oat sacks were strewn over an area of a couple of dozen square yards. Canned goods were scattered around, covered with syrup and dirt.

"That your bear, Kirk?" Eli Yockey asked gruffly.

Kirk nodded. "I turned him loose."

Shorty limped back into the circle of light, his face a mask of rage. His clothes were torn and his hands and face were scratched and dirty. A man standing in the darkness asked, "Who beat the hell out of who, Shorty?"

The 3Y man swung around. "Who said that?"

Nobody answered, but there was more than one hidden, sly grin in the crowd.

Eli Yockey broke the tension by turning to Kirk. "We'll kill that bear of yours if we see him again. It ain't too big a step from raidin' camp to killin' calves."

Kirk nodded gravely. "I can't blame you." The bear would have to take his chances now just as any other wild thing would.

Shorty was eyeing Kirk balefully. As the crowd began drifting away, Shorty said, "You was with Rachel a hell of a long time. I suppose you took her all the way home."

Kirk met Shorty's stare steadily, knowing that the man was hoping to prod him into a fight so that to Eli and the others it would appear to be Kirk's fault. He said softly between his teeth, "Now, Shorty? You want it now?"

Shorty's face grew livid with fury. His great hands trembled as they clenched and unclenched. He said, "I'll pick my time." Then he turned and strode furiously to the cabin and went inside.

The lantern had been left on the ground. By its light Kirk cleaned up the mess the bear had made. Then, instead of leaving the storeroom open as it had been before, he closed the door and slipped a stick into the padlock hasp.

59

Picking up the lantern, he went to the cabin. He jacked up the chimney, blew the flame out, and went inside. Silence greeted him. He got out of his clothes in the darkness and crawled into his bunk. He lay staring at the ceiling for a few moments, briefly wondering what excuse Shorty would drum up tomorrow to justify a fight. Then he went to sleep.

He was up with the others at dawn. He glanced around the room, wondering where Shorty had gone. He didn't have to wait long for his answer. As he stepped outside for his turn at the spring, he saw a fresh-killed steer carcass hanging from the main ridgepole that extended out in front of the cabin. On the ground beside it was the steer's hide, carelessly but deliberately arranged so the brand would show. It was Tomahawk.

It was clear to Kirk that Shorty planned to make Kirk begin the fight, so Shorty himself would not be blamed for it by Eli and the others. At the same time Shorty had arranged it so that no one could say he had fought because of jealousy over Rachel.

Anger stirred in Kirk as he considered the underhandedness of Shorty's method. The 3Y foreman wanted to make this something more than an excuse for a fight. He wanted to show Kirk up, wanted to demonstrate clearly to all the Salt Creek men that Kirk was still loyal to Tomahawk, and that he could not be trusted in the coming crisis.

Eli Yockey came out of the cabin, saw the hide, glanced quickly at Kirk, and hurried toward the spring.

Kirk stood there, frowning. Killing Tomahawk beef for camp-meat was a common practice among the Salt Creek ranchers and had been for years. Guy was aware of it, but he'd never been able to catch them at it. Kirk knew that his father would give a hundred dollars to get his hands on this piece of evidence.

Reluctantly Kirk turned and headed for the spring. It went against his grain to ignore the hide, but he didn't have much choice. Filing and pressing a rustling complaint right now would blow the country wide open. It could cost a dozen lives.

He washed in the icy water of the spring, and returned to the cabin. Most of the men now squatted immediately before it, smoking and waiting for breakfast. Eli was cooking this

60

morning, and Shorty was among those in front of the cabin.

Shorty looked up as Kirk approached, an expression of savage triumph in his eyes. Kirk ignored him and rolled a smoke. Shorty said, "I got up early an' went huntin'. Had some luck, too."

Kirk said nothing, feeling his muscles knot and knowing that the long threatened finish fight was here.

Shorty wouldn't let it lie. He said, "A man must be pretty damn gutless to shut his eyes when somebody kills his beef."

Kirk stood up and tossed his cigarette away. "All right, Shorty," he said. "You've been wanting a fight and now you're going to get it. But it's not over that beef hanging there because it isn't my beef." He looked at Luke Bartram and Chet Tappan and the rest. "I'm not fighting for Tomahawk. You savvy that? This is personal."

Shorty got up and ground out his cigarette stub under his boot. He crouched a little as he moved toward Kirk. Kirk said, "We're not in a prize ring. This is no-holds-barred all the way."

"Suits me," Shorty said, and kept moving forward.

Kirk backed up from Shorty's advance, but as he passed the hanging carcass, he seized it by a foreleg and yanked it with him. Then he released it, giving it a violent push toward Shorty. Swinging like a monstrous pendulum, it struck Shorty and knocked him off his feet.

Kirk followed the swinging carcass, but Shorty rolled away from him toward the cabin wall. Kirk landed on the ground with his knees. He started to get up. The carcass caught him in the butt on its second swing and drove him head first into Shorty's body. They piled up in a squirming tangle, each trying to get on top.

There was immense strength in Shorty's thick arms. Quick fear touched Kirk, for he knew what would happen if Shorty ever caught him in his great arms and squeezed. He brought a knee into Shorty's groin. The muscles in Shorty's arms relaxed and Kirk rolled away. His hand, falling to one side, encountered the steer's hide.

Shorty came up with a double-bitted ax in his hands, one which had been leaning against the cabin wall. Raw fury was in his eyes, and Kirk saw something else there, too. It was more than fury; it was a murderous rage. Shorty wanted to kill. Kirk hadn't realized this before, and the knowledge struck him with a shock.

Shorty swung the ax back over his shoulder. Panic gripped Kirk briefly. That ax would swing in a five-foot arc. There wasn't anywhere he could go to avoid it.

The hide was under his hands. Kirk heard the other men shout, with Eli's voice rising above the others, "No! Shorty, drop that ax!"

But Shorty didn't hear. Kirk saw the man's great biceps tense. He saw the ax begin its swing.

Kirk seized the hide with both hands. Heavy and green, it shed a shower of blood as he flung it out. The ax head bit into it and was stopped as suddenly as if it had struck a tree. Then the partly opened hide hit Shorty in the face.

Kirk was up, following it. He struck Shorty with the point of his shoulder, his hands reaching again for the hide. As Shorty went back, Kirk went with him, clawing at the hide, spreading it over Shorty's head and face.

Shorty struggled, trying to rid himself of the hide. Kirk kneed him savagely in the belly. He had the hide spread over the upper half of Shorty's body and across his face.

Shorty whipped his thick body around violently, trying to get out from under the hide. But Kirk held it in place, absorbing the rain of awkward blows from Shorty's fists, the brutal kicks of his booted feet. Shorty's chest heaved, but he wasn't getting any air. Gradually his struggles weakened.

"Kirk, get that off him," Eli yelled. "You tryin' to kill him?"

Kirk glared at Eli. "What do you think he was trying to do to me with that ax?"

But he got up, and watched while Shorty fought free of the hide. His face was slick with blood and hair from the hide. His great chest worked like a bellows. He got to his feet slowly, his little eyes switching around until he saw the ax. He made a lunge toward it, but he never got his hand on it. Kirk hit him on the nose. Blood sprayed down Shorty's chin and chest. Kirk followed with a sledging right, this one striking Shorty's left cheekbone.

Shorty made no attempt to retaliate. He seemed to be unable to think of anything except getting his hands on the ax again. He turned aside and stooped. Kirk brought his two clasped and knotted hands down on the back of his neck like a club.

The blow drove Shorty's face down into the dirt, but still his hands clawed out, half consciously, for the ax handle. Kirk brought a boot down on one of his wrists, then stepped back and kicked the ax away.

Shorty rolled over on his back and stared at the sky. He was breathing gustily and noisily because of the blood in his throat. His eyes were glazed.

"All right," Eli said as if he was disappointed in the way the fight had ended. "That's all. Get a bucket of water, somebody."

Kirk stood spread-legged and exhausted, his own breathing like the rasp of a file. He looked at the men around him, turning slowly, his gaze pinned on Luke Bartram's face. Bartram was Shorty's best friend and the man most likely to pick up his fight.

Bartram stared at the ground. No one said a word. Kirk tramped wearily to the spring, his mind feeling as though it were drugged. But a single thought seeped through: *He tried to kill me with that ax. He'll keep trying until one of us is dead.*

Ten

In the days that followed his fight with Shorty Hough, Kirk discovered that the man's defeat had settled nothing. Indeed, it seemed to have increased the resentment felt by the Salt Creek crowd toward him.

Kirk became acutely conscious that in spite of his working with them, living with them, in spite of his flat statements that he was one of them and had no further connection with Tomahawk, they still considered him an outsider and even an enemy. The feeling was natural enough, he thought with some bitterness. He was a Van Horn, and Eli and Luke Bartram and several more had suffered at the hands of Guy Van Horn.

They rode Buck Point, a strip of land varying from one

to five miles wide and ten miles long. They were in their saddles from dawn to dark, scattering the cattle, putting out salt at selected locations to keep them scattered. Many of the springs had dried up, making their task more difficult. Since there was not enough grass for the cattle to eat, they drifted more than they ordinarily would have done.

Each day the tension increased. The small amount of feed on Buck Point might sustain the cattle for a couple of weeks without too much danger of loss. If it didn't rain, Kirk knew that two weeks' respite was all Guy could hope for. After that the Salt Creek ranchers would have to move in on Tomahawk or watch their cattle die.

Fights among the Salt Creekers themselves were frequent. And Eli Yockey's face grew more and more worried with each passing day. He therefore welcomed the news, brought by Rachel on Friday, that there would be a dance in the Salt Creek schoolhouse on Saturday.

"Maybe a good shindig will ease things up," he told Kirk.

Kirk refused Rachel's invitation to see her off the mountain, and wondered at his motives for doing so. A few weeks ago he would have welcomed such a chance to be alone with her. He wasn't afraid of Shorty. He'd beaten the man once. He guessed, grinning wryly to himself, that he was as afraid of Rachel as anyone. He wasn't ready to marry and she was.

Kirk left the cow camp on Buck Point at noon Saturday with the Salt Creek men, all of them in high spirits for the first time since roundup began. Kirk rode with the others as far as the 3Y where they separated, each going to his own home. Kirk reached his place in late afternoon.

Carrying a clean suit of underwear, he went to the creek and bathed in its icy water. After that he shaved in a cracked mirror hung on the outside wall of his cabin. Then he dressed in his last clean pair of jeans and his last clean shirt. He'd have to return to Tomahawk soon to pick up the rest of his clothes.

His thoughts turned to the dance and he found himself anticipating it, as much for the fact that he'd see his brothers and Bianca and the Tomahawk crew as for the dancing itself. He hesitated about his gun, uncertain whether to take it or not. Finally he hung the holster and belt on the wall and stuffed the gun under his belt.

He cooked a quick meal of venison steak and potatoes, then saddled and took the road for the schoolhouse, located four miles down country from his cabin at the foot of the Tomahawk trail which came directly off the plateau north of the Buck Point fence.

He arrived in early dusk. There were a few rigs already at the schoolhouse, those of the families who would make it ready: sweep the floor, light the lamps, and spread the dancing wax. The women were inside taking care of those chores, and the men were hunkered against the log wall of the schoolhouse, smoking and talking. They looked at Kirk without friendliness as he came up, and thereafter did not include him in their conversation.

The lines were drawn, he thought, and he was a maverick. He wondered if the time would ever come when he would be accepted, if they would ever forget he was a Van Horn.

So he waited while the sky grew dark. More rigs arrived, and finally the Tomahawk crew rode in on horseback, bringing Bianca Chavez with them.

Kirk got up and went to her at once. She stood beside her horse, talking to Matt and Billy. Kirk did not see Guy. That didn't surprise him: Guy seldom came to these dances.

The way Bianca's eyes lighted when she saw Kirk warmed his heart after the unfriendliness and hostility he'd experienced at the hands of the Salt Creek people these last days. She put out both hands and he took them, finding them cold and trembling.

"Howdy, Bee," he said. "I want every third dance."

Her smile was quick and genuine. "I promise, Kirk."

He turned to Matt, taking his brother's big hand. "How are things going, Matt?"

"All right, I guess, but it sure ain't the same without you."

"How's Guy?"

Matt smiled wearily. "Stormin' and raisin' hell just like always."

Frank Surrency called, "Kirk, come here."

Kirk grinned at Bianca and walked to where Surrency stood beside his horse. The cowboy reached into the saddlebags and brought out a flat quart bottle. "Have a drink, Kirk."

Kirk tipped the bottle. He wiped his mouth with the back of his hand and looked at Surrency, a half smile on his lips.

He said, "Behave yourself tonight, Frank. No fights. Tell the others, will you?"

"Sure, Kirk." But there was a stubborn, almost defiant light in Surrency's dark eyes, as though he had qualified his promise with "Unless they start something."

The fiddle inside the hall squalled, and then the small orchestra struck up a lively tune. Men began drifting through the front door of the schoolhouse.

Shorty Hough claimed Rachel for the first dance. Turning, Kirk found Bianca beside him. He put an arm around her and swung her onto the floor. The Salt Creek dances hadn't changed during the five years he'd been gone, he thought. There was always a great deal of stomping and whirling, both the men and women dancing with the enthusiasm of people finding escape from the dreary monotony of life if only for a few hours.

Kirk and Bianca danced past the long table set against the back wall. The box suppers were on top of the table, and underneath were the clothesbaskets in which the small children were sleeping. The Tappan baby woke and began to cry. Mrs. Tappan left her husband, and hurrying to her baby, picked him up.

Kirk was always surprised when he danced with Bianca. She was as light as a goose feather, anticipating his every move. With some women he felt awkward, but never with Bianca. Any man could dance with her, he thought.

Her elfin face was tipped up toward him as she watched him with peculiar intensity. She asked, "How have you been, Kirk? You're thinner."

"Maybe. Delfino all right?"

She smiled at that. "Dad's always all right. He's the only thing in this crazy world that never changes."

Kirk glanced across the room to where Shorty and Rachel were dancing. They were of equal height. She was smiling at Shorty and talking, but Shorty's face held the scowling expression that was habitual with him these days. She caught Kirk's eyes and her smile faded.

Kirk felt a twinge of guilt. He should have asked her for the first dance, he supposed. Women were funny about things like that. The dance ended, and Frank Surrency was

66

there instantly to take Bianca. She watched Kirk as she whirled away.

He knew he should claim Rachel from Shorty. But perversely he didn't. Instead, he crossed the floor and took Marge Yockey, Eli's wife, out of gaunt Lew Warren's arms.

"Go find your own wife, Lew," Kirk said. "You can't have Marge all night." As they danced away, he looked down at Eli's wife thinking that in many ways her life was a hard one. She was Rachel's stepmother and only a few months older.

"Nice dance," Kirk said.

She was light in his arms, as excited and happy as a girl. Impulsively she hugged Kirk. "A wonderful dance," she said. "I've been looking forward to it all week."

He caught Rachel's glance again across the room. Her anger was growing by the minute, he thought. Kirk turned his head, disturbed, not entirely sure why he was avoiding Rachel except that he had been uneasy with her from the moment she'd asked that question about their getting married. The next time he saw her, she was talking to Shorty again, and Shorty's scowl was deeper than it had been before.

Rachel had watched Kirk dance away with Bianca as the music started. Irritated, she had nevertheless realized that he probably had been unable to avoid Bianca. But she could think of no excuse for him when he deliberately went out and claimed her stepmother from Lew Warren, and her anger rose.

Impelled by that emotion, she said to Shorty, "That must have been quite a fight you had with Kirk. I hear he mopped up the cow camp with you."

"He got me tangled up in a green hide."

"A Tomahawk hide?"

"How'd you know?"

"I know you. Was that what the fight was about?"

He was silent a moment, glowering; then he said, "You know well enough what we was fightin' about. You."

Rachel felt a pleasant tingle run through her body. It was heady stuff, having two men fighting over her. And yet, looking at Shorty, she felt a twinge of guilt and fear. He had changed since Kirk had bought the K Bar. From an ordinary, hard-working man, he had become a savage and unpredictable one. He was dangerous. Eli had told her about the ax.

Her glance went across the room and found Kirk again. He was laughing and looking down into Marge's eyes. He had no right to dance with Marge, she thought angrily, and leave her with Shorty. In a burst of spite, she said, "I guess a girl can never trust a man, can she?"

"What you talking about?" His voice was more ominous than she had ever heard it. He followed her glance which was resting on Kirk. "What do you mean? Has he . . ."

"It's only that . . ." She flushed, avoiding his eyes. She knew she was handling this wrong, but now that she had started, she couldn't turn back. "Well, Kirk as much as proposed to me the other night, and now . . ."

She stopped. Shorty's voice was deadly. "What happened? Did he take advantage of you?" he demanded.

She felt his shoulder muscles tighten under her hand, and she knew that his hand at her back had clenched into a fist. Suddenly the full significance of what she had done struck her. Alarmed, she said, "Shorty, don't start anything. Please! You'd turn the dance into a brawl; the whole Tomahawk crew's here."

He didn't answer her. Her alarm grew when she saw how he looked at her. She said again, "Shorty, don't start anything." Still he said nothing, and when the dance ended, he stomped away from her without a backward glance. He disappeared in the crowd. A moment later she saw him go through the door with Lew Warren, presumably to get a bottle from Lew's rig.

Rachel looked around, her alarm giving way to something close to panic. Shorty, cold sober, was dangerous enough. Drunk, he was infinitely more so. Her eyes found Bianca in the crowd, but Kirk was nowhere to be seen. She hurried toward Bianca, fear such a pressure in her chest that she found it hard to breathe. She knew Shorty carried a gun under his belt. She had felt it when she'd been dancing with him. She didn't know whether Kirk had one or not.

She thrust herself through the crowd until she reached Bianca. She said breathlessly, "Bianca, I've got to talk to you."

Bianca looked at her, making no attempt to hide her dislike. "What about?"

"About Kirk and Shorty. We've got to do something. Kirk's in danger."

Concern showed in Bianca's eyes. "What happened?"

Rachel glanced around at the crowd. She said, her voice lowered, "Shorty's jealous. He's got a gun. He's crazy."

"Kirk hasn't been near you all evening," Bianca said suspiciously. "Why should Shorty be jealous?"

"I was mad." Rachel couldn't meet the other girl's eyes. "I told Shorty something I should have kept to myself."

Bianca stared at her. "What do you want me to do?"

"Get Kirk and the Tomahawk boys to leave. Right away. It's the only way to save Kirk's life."

"Or Shorty's. So you tried to sic Shorty on to Kirk like one dog on another?" Bianca said hotly.

"That's not fair!" Rachel cried.

"Fair?" Bianca said scornfully. "What do you know about what's fair? You let Kirk alone after this. He's got enough trouble without you making things worse."

Turning, Bianca ran the length of the schoolhouse and through the door. Rachel watched her go. She listened, waiting for the sound of a shot outside. Tension built in her until she felt as if she had to scream.

Leaning against the wall, trembling, Rachel lifted her eyes. She whispered, "Oh God, don't let Kirk be hurt."

She heard shouts outside, but she couldn't tell whether they were angry ones or not. A moment later she heard the drum of many hoofs on the hard-packed ground.

Relief weakened her knees so that she had to sit down on one of the benches that lined the wall. Bianca had succeeded. Kirk and the Tomahawk riders had left, but had Kirk gone because of his feeling for Bianca? Rachel was sure Bianca was in love with Kirk. She had seen it in the girl's eyes, sensed it in the way she talked.

Rachel clenched her fists. Bianca couldn't have him! Rachel wouldn't let that happen . . . Kirk—and Tomahawk—belonged to her.

Shaking, she put her head down into her hands. Bloodshed had been averted for tonight. But what about tomorrow? And the day after that? Silently she began to cry.

Eleven

The usual spring rains did not come to the White River coun
try, not even by the time spring roundup was finished or
Tomahawk and the ranch had settled down to its regular routine. In May the plateau was as barren as it had been in mid-
winter, or nearly so. Grass, usually started much earlier than
this by melting snow and early rains, failed to come, or when
it did, dried and died before it got more than an inch high.

Wind, still dry and cold, rattled the loose boards around
the Tomahawk buildings, banged doors shut and picked up
empty buckets to send them rolling and clanging across the
dusty yard. Tempers, already sharpened by drought, became
honed to a fine edge by the endless chilling wind.

Dust, lifted from the parched land in great, spiraling clouds,
made a constant grating between men's teeth and was an irri-
tating rasp against their skins. And worst of all, there was
no prospect of change in the weather. Even the pine needles
and dry leaves from the previous year crackled underfoot,
making the danger of fire a constant, haunting menace.

Matt rode in late one night from the Cathedral Rim cow
camp, his eyes red-rimmed from dust and wind. When he
came down for breakfast, he said worriedly, "I don't know
what's going to happen to that Salt Creek bunch, Pa. There's
nothin' on Buck Point! Nothin' at all. It's like a desert."

"I ain't going to worry about them," Guy growled. "Tomahawk's got worries enough of its own."

Kate brought a platter of flapjacks from the stove and set
them down in front of him. She said with asperity, "Tomahawk might be a sight better off if you *did* worry about 'em."

Guy bent over his plate, refusing to dignify her protest
with an answer. Tessie's death had been a shock to him that
he'd thought would never grow less painful. Time had dulled
the sharpness of it, but missing her was a steady ache that
refused to heal with the passage of time. He had supposed it
would be that way, but he hadn't known it would be this bad.
He often caught himself thinking of her as he rode toward

home, and then he would realize she wasn't there. Whenever he did, the pain became almost intolerable.

The bitter truth was that Tessie had made him a full, whole man. She had been like deep, still water, giving strength to him when he needed it, giving purpose just by being here at Tomahawk doing the things she had always done.

Guy's sense of guilt was a festering sore that remained raw and open. He knew now that he could have done many things for her; he could have given her many things to ease her burdens. The truth was, giving her things had simply not occurred to him. The habit of thrift, born in the years of hardship and growth, had been too strong. And Tessie had not been one to ask for anything, or, he supposed, even to care for the things most women cherished.

But Kate, now, was the exact opposite of Tessie. She not only asked for things; she demanded them. And fighting her was like fighting a feather mattress. It gave and folded around you, but when you withdrew, you found that it had already fluffed back into its original shape.

He soon discovered that it was easier to give in to Kate than to oppose her. She hounded him until he had the living room cleaned out, and his complaint that he didn't have a place to store anything only brought her acid "Then build a place! I don't give a damn where you put the stuff. Just get it to hell out of here. And another thing—you can send a wagon to town and buy me a rocker."

He'd blown up over that, but she'd replied as calmly and adamantly as though she'd asked for nothing, "It's a hell of a note when a body has to go to bed to rest, or sit in a straight-backed chair till their back aches. When I'm through washing your clothes and cleaning your house, I aim to sit on the front porch in a rocking chair." She waggled her forefinger at him. "If you'd done a few things like that for Tessie. . . ."

"Shut up," he yelled. "Shut up!"

But the next morning he'd sent Frank Surrency to Jubilee in the wagon and told him to buy a rocking chair that would hold Kate's bulk. Now he felt like kicking the damned thing every time he walked past it. It was a symbol of his defeat at the hands of a woman. And though he knew he couldn't get along without her, he resented her more bitterly than ever, and planned ways in which he could get rid of her and emerge triumphant.

Yet in his calmer moments, he was grudgingly grateful for what she did. She kept his house spotless and cooked the meals, and washed and mended his and the boys' clothes.

This morning, as Guy rose from the table, Kate said, "Don't go yet. I want to talk to you."

She waited until Matt and Billy left the kitchen. Guy glanced at her, uneasy, wondering what it would be this time.

He'd never quarreled with Tessie, but it seemed he couldn't be in the same room with Kate five minutes without quarreling. And he didn't enjoy quarreling, particularly not since Tessie's death. Maybe it was because he didn't feel well lately. His head ached almost continually with great, skull-shaking throbs that nothing seemed to help.

He dropped resignedly back into his chair as he said irritably, "If you're going to keep me here, fetch me some more coffee."

She obeyed, then sat down across the table from him. She said, "Guy, I want you to send for Kirk."

He opened his mouth to shout something at her. That had always been his method, simply to roar down any opposition, but Kate couldn't be handled that way. She glared at him so fiercely that he closed his mouth.

She went on implacably, "You need Kirk. I've been watching you and I know you're not well. You shouldn't do as much as you do."

Again he started to speak, but she silenced him with "Shut up and listen till I'm done."

He subsided, wondering at himself. Kate said, "Besides that, Kirk doesn't belong on Salt Creek. I don't like that bunch any more than you do. They're sly and greedy and small. They're not our kind of people and they're not Kirk's, either. He belongs here, with you and his own brothers. Tessie'd have wanted it that way and you know it."

Guy's head started to pound as rage built up in him. He started to shout, then calmed his voice with an effort. "I'll never send for Kirk! He made his damned bed when he rode out the day of the funeral—when he said his home was on Salt Creek. All right, let him rot down there."

Kate said bitterly, "You pigheaded fool! Can't you see that you made him say that? When did you ever give him a chance to be a man? Did you want to do to Kirk what you've done to Matt? And what you're doing to Billy?"

Guy couldn't meet her eyes. He knew she was right. He remembered how close he had once been to Kirk. He could have kept that relationship if he'd tried. Now, thinking back, he knew he just hadn't tried.

But he couldn't admit that Kate was right and he was wrong. And he couldn't degrade himself by asking Kirk to come back.

Kirk *would* be a lot of help. Kate was right in that. He was a good worker, and he had more cow savvy than any hired man Guy had ever had. More than Matt would ever have, or Billy, either, probably. Guy wondered about Billy, wondered if he'd turn out to have as much grit in his craw as Kirk had.

Guy finished his coffee. Kate's tirade had changed nothing. Kirk had made his decision. Guy asked harshly, "That all?"

"It's enough, isn't it? You going to send for him?"

"No!"

Guy rose. Kate said angrily, "I can't see for the life of me how a man can be so smart on some things and so damned stupid on others! All you've got to do to stop trouble is to give that Salt Creek bunch a little grass."

"I'll handle any trouble when it comes," Guy said, and stamped out of the house.

He crossed the yard to the corral. The crew had ridden out. Matt and Billy were gone, too, Matt back to the cow camp and Billy out to pack salt to the bulls in the hayfields. Guy put a hand against a corral bar to steady himself. Unfamiliar tremors ran through his body; his head pounded without mercy. A new, unaccustomed dizziness bothered him this morning, but if he waited here a minute, it would go away. He was sure of that.

He looked out across the hay meadows and wondered if there would be enough water in Beaver Creek this summer to irrigate properly. There always had been, but this was the worst drought he'd seen in all the years he'd been here. He'd make out, though. He had enough hay carried over from previous years to get through the winter, and enough dry grass on the range to pull his cattle through.

He rubbed his eyes, wishing he could do something to get rid of his headache. He wasn't old enough to be sick. But age didn't seem to have much to do with the way a man felt. What good was all his wealth when his head seemed ready to explode, when he had to hang onto a corral bar to stand up?

He considered going into the house and lying down, but he didn't want to have to explain to Kate. Besides, the habit of working during the daylight hours was too strong.

Eventually the dizziness passed. He took his rope from the corral post and caught his bay gelding, the one he usually rode. For a moment he stood beside the horse, absently combing the tangles out of his mane with his fingers. The bay nuzzled him and he patted the animal's neck. Maybe if he could sleep better . . . he hadn't had a good night's sleep since Tessie died. . . .

He wondered bleakly what his lifetime of hard work had really accomplished. He'd lost his wife. Now he'd lost his oldest boy. He had Kate Gorman in the house bullying him constantly, telling him what to do.

He turned and saw the rocking chair on the front porch. Suddenly he felt a wild fury that started blood to pounding in his head again. Damn that chair! Sometime he'd take an ax and make kindling out of it. Maybe then Kate would go back where she belonged.

He saddled up and rode along Beaver Creek. He'd have a look at the upper meadow where a couple of men were irrigating. He had to get away from here, had to quit thinking about Tessie.

He was discovering a weakness in himself he'd never dreamed was there. It was a weakness to look back with regret, and Guy Van Horn hated weakness. A man worth his salt took what he wanted.

Suddenly he reined up, startled. Billy's little mouse-colored mare was standing by the creek, her reins dragging. The pack horse, its panniers loaded with salt, stood nearby, tied to a willow shoot. Guy realized with relief that Billy wasn't hurt, or he wouldn't have tied the pack horse. And then beyond the mare, he saw Billy standing on the bank, fishing, so intent he hadn't heard his father's approach.

Anger smoldered in Guy, and it swelled as the moments passed. You tried to raise a boy to have some regard for work and responsibility, but the minute your back was turned, this was what he did. . . .

He walked toward Billy, careful not to make any noise. The boy had cut a willow pole and was using a hair from the mare's tail for a leader. Guy supposed he'd carried the hook and line concealed beneath the sweat band of his hat.

Billy's body was tense. He stood close to the bank, bending over the water. The pole was in his right hand, and the baited hook had swept downstream to the edge of a dark mass of willow roots that extended halfway across the creek. Just as Guy reached for the boy, Billy had a strike. He jerked the pole up, yanking out a gleaming, dripping ten-inch trout.

Guy ducked involuntarily, but the fish struck him on the shoulder. Turning, Billy saw his father. He started to run, but Guy, lunging toward him, caught him by his shirt.

All the day's suppressed fury burst loose in Guy. His face was livid and the veins in his forehead throbbed. He shouted, "By God, how many times have I got to tell you about fishin' when you've got work to do?"

The boy struggled and tried to break free. Guy's anger rose and broke. He roared, "Get this through your head! During workin' hours, you work! After that what you do is your own affair."

Billy continued to struggle, frantic with fear. He kicked his father on the shin just above the top of his cowhide boot. Pain shot up Guy's leg. He stumbled, his grip relaxing. Billy jerked free and ran for his mare.

Guy took a single step in pursuit. Then his knees buckled and he fell, slipping down the bank. He splashed as he hit the water. He lay motionless, his upper body on the bank, his thighs and legs in the icy creek.

Terror and panic gripped his mind. He couldn't move. He tried to speak, but no sound came from his lips. His hat fell off his head. For the first time since he'd been a baby, Guy Van Horn was completely helpless.

He lay there hour after hour, conscious, but not thinking

clearly. The sun climbed until it was noon-high, its glare blinding. It added little heat to the biting wind that stirred the willows along the bank, yet he felt no cold.

But he could hear. The rustle of the water was a constant sound. Someone galloped past shortly after noon. The beat of hoofs was faint at first, grew louder, then faded and died. Birds flew close and perched on willow branches, chirping cheerfully, then flew away in fright when they saw Guy. An occasional cottontail rattled the dry leaves under the willows. From somewhere out in the meadow a lark's clear, sweet song came to him.

Guy had no idea what had happened. He'd felt no pain. Yet no amount of will or desire could move a muscle of his body. He could see and hear, but the power of speech and motion was gone.

Mentally he cursed Billy, cursed the boy's fear of him that had made him leave. Why didn't somebody come? He needed care; he needed Doc Peters now as he'd never needed him before. But nobody knew he was here. Maybe nobody gave a damn . . . the thought was startling and painful.

Shadows along the creek lengthened and the wind increased, sighing noisily among the willows. Then he heard something coming. Or was it somebody? Again he tried to cry out, to move, to do anything that would attract attention. But it was no use.

The sounds came closer. Fear struck through him. A bear had stopped directly over him, so close he could smell the animal's hot breath in his face.

Once his first paralyzing fright was gone, Guy recognized Eli, the boys' tame bear. Yet even recognizing the bear did not reassure him. Eli hated him. He was sure of it. Eli would claw and maul him. He'd tear an arm loose from its socket; he'd pick him up in his monstrous mouth and shake him the way a dog shakes a rat to death.

For what seemed like hours Eli sat there on his haunches drooling into his face. The damned bear was grinning at him and dripping at the mouth like a small boy at a candy counter. What the devil was he waiting for?

Delirium touched Guy's mind. It wasn't the bear at all sitting here. If it had been, he'd have torn Guy apart long

76

ago. It was Eli Yockey, without a hat, his hair black with shoe polish.

Eli Yockey was sitting here laughing at him, mocking him because now Eli could move in and seize Tomahawk. The boys couldn't hold it. Guy hadn't taught them to.

Eli's tiny eyes seemed triumphant. Guy knew what he was thinking. *So you drove us off the plateau. You crowded us onto Buck Point because you were stronger than we were. But now we're coming back. Now we're coming back. . . .*

Guy lost consciousness then, his last memory that of the bear's, or the man's, face right over his, inches away. His last thought was one of defeat. With Guy helpless the Salt Creek bunch could move in and take anything they wanted. No one would be here to stop them. Even Kirk, who might have stopped them, wouldn't be here to do it.

This was the pay-off. This was the end of Tomahawk.

Twelve

When Billy Van Horn jerked free from his father, he was in the grip of panic. He had seen something in his father's face that he'd never seen before, a fury that had turned Guy's face almost purple. It had made Billy desperate to get away.

He looked back once and saw that his father had fallen. He'd never seen Guy helpless or unconscious before. Seeing him lying motionless now multiplied his fear. He supposed his father had stumbled and struck his head as he fell. But he'd be up soon enough, and when he was . . .

Billy rode his mare to where the pack horse was tied. Without dismounting, he untied the halter rope from the willow. Leading the pack animal, he rode to where Guy's bay stood cropping grass, and gathered up the gelding's reins. Then, leading both horses, he rode away.

After he had gone a mile, he dismounted, tied up the bay's reins, and turned him loose. The gelding would go straight home and Guy would have the horse if he needed him.

Billy put out the blocks of salt where Guy wanted them,

then tied the halter rope to the packsaddle and turned this horse loose, too. After that he rode aimlessly upcountry toward the plateau top, his direction roughly southwest. He couldn't force himself to go home. He had disobeyed his father before, but he'd never fought to escape his punishment. He didn't know why he had today. Wondering, he remembered the expression he'd seen on his father's face.

At noon he was hungry, but he didn't want to ride into one of the cow camps. He didn't want to see anyone. He even ducked a couple of Tomahawk riders who were ahead of him, swung due west and rode through a bunch of quakies, heading directly toward Cathedral Rim.

A dozen ideas worked through Billy's mind, all of them about ways of getting out of the country. His father didn't really hate him, he was sure of that, but Billy knew anything could happen when he went into a rage as he had today.

Right now Billy wasn't certain of his own feelings. Maybe he hated his father. It must have been that way with Kirk five years ago, he thought. And Kirk had left, and had come back a grown man not afraid to stand up to his father. . . .

Daydreaming, Billy imagined himself like Kirk, and for a time the thought strengthened him. His jaw thrust forward. He wasn't going home. If he didn't, there was only one thing left to do. Get out of the country, like Kirk had. Billy wondered where he'd get a job. He wasn't strong enough for a man's work. Maybe he could find an outfit big enough to hire a chore boy.

He had no money. Guy never gave him any. He didn't own a gun, so he couldn't even kill a rabbit for his supper. He'd have to beg a meal from some ranch, and except for Tomahawk, the closest ranches were on Salt Creek. The way things were, Billy doubted if anyone down there would give him a meal.

Another thought suddenly drove a cold spasm of fear clear down to the bottom of his belly. He didn't own the mare he was riding. When Guy came to, he'd notify Red Henessy, the sheriff.

Billy began to tremble. Henessy would get him if it took all summer. Henessy was a regular bloodhound on anything like this, and he'd ride around the world to do a job for Guy.

Billy had no doubts about what would happen to him when he was caught. Henessy would throw him in jail.

His thinking went fuzzy. He was so hungry he felt weak. And he'd let imaginary fears build up until he wasn't able to make a clear decision. He just couldn't see any way out.

Swinging north, he struck Red Creek and crossed it. The sun was down, but he was hardly conscious of that. By the time he hit the trail between Tomahawk and the Cathedral Rim cow camp, darkness was complete.

Weariness and hunger were overpowering forces in him. He moved into a thick grove of quakies and dismounted. He tied the little mare securely, and lay down upon the ground, raking a pile of dead leaves together for a pillow. He stared at the sky for a moment, and suddenly he was sound asleep.

When he awoke, the moon was high in the sky. He had absolutely no idea what time it was, but from the position of the moon he knew several hours had passed while he slept. He was thirsty and ravenously hungry. The rest had cleared his mind. He knew he had to find Kirk. Kirk was the only one who could help him now.

He mounted, turned into the trail and let his horse have its head. The plateau was alive with the weird, cold moonlight upon it. Every cedar seemed to be an animate, menacing thing; every coyote call became the cry of a wolf leading the pack to him.

He thought once that he saw a bear ahead of him in the trail and wondered if it was Eli or a wild bear on the hunt. He made a wide circle, then returned to the trail, fearing the mare's reaction if she should scent the bear.

And then, half a mile from the cow camp, he heard riders coming. Instinctively he pulled off the trail into the shadow of a clump of cedars. There he sat his saddle, rigid, while the fears that had plagued him all day returned to his mind. Not until the riders had reached him and gone past did he recognize Kirk and Matt.

With near-hysterical relief, he called out, "Kirk! Kirk!"

Kirk and Matt pulled up their horses and turned as he came rocketing along the trail to them. Kirk said incredulously, "Billy! What the hell are you doing way out here?"

Billy pulled up, his hands folded on the saddle horn, so

79

weak with relief that for a moment he couldn't talk. Kirk rode to him and laid a hand on his shoulder.

"What is it, boy? Where've you been all day? Matt said you were missing."

"I've been ridin'." Billy swallowed, fighting back the sobs that were gathering in his throat. He had the crazy notion that he was dreaming this. Kirk was down on Buck Point with the Salt Creek bunch, and Matt was at home this time of night. But he felt Kirk's big, reassuring hand on his shoulder and he heard Kirk's voice, "Why are you so late getting home? Don't you know it's 'way past midnight?"

Billy blurted out what had happened, the words coming in bursts that were almost incoherent at times. Then he asked frantically, "What am I goin' to do, Kirk? I couldn't figure it out. I was headed for Buck Point to find you."

Kirk said in a tired, cranky voice. "Damn Pa's ornery soul anyway! You had a right to be scared. Come on, let's ride. I'll tell you what happened as we go."

They went on toward Tomahawk. Matt dropped behind to allow Kirk and Billy to ride abreast. Kirk said, "When Pa's horse got home, Kate thought he'd been throwed, and he'd come limping in before long. She waited till after noon and he didn't show up, so she started looking for him. She missed him when she went past, and had to backtrack. It was getting along toward dark when she finally found him where you'd been fishing. Eli was bending over him. She shooed the bear off and then found out Pa'd had a stroke. She got him home and sent Matt after me, and Frank Surrency after Doc."

Billy's voice was a scared whisper when he asked, "Is he pretty bad?"

"Damn bad," Matt said from behind them. "He can't move. He can't even talk."

Kirk said sharply, "It's not your fault, Billy. Don't start thinking it is. If Pa hadn't let himself get so worked up, it wouldn't have happened. It's like the rest of the trouble that comes to him—it's his own doing. And Kate's more worried about you than she is about Pa. She figured you'd be back by noon at the latest."

After that they rode in silence. Billy was ashamed of his feelings, but he couldn't help being relieved. Maybe Kirk would stay and run Tomahawk. Everything would be different if he did. Billy didn't know anything about strokes, but Matt said Guy could neither move nor talk.

Presently the lights of Tomahawk showed ahead of them. Billy couldn't stand the uncertainty any longer, so he blurted out, "You going to stay here, Kirk?"

"He'll have to," Matt said from where he rode behind.

Kirk didn't answer immediately. It occurred to Billy that Matt was as scared of their father as he was. Kirk was the only one who wasn't afraid, but Kirk was different from him and Matt. He'd been different all his life and that was why he'd gone away. Billy had been only ten then, but he remembered. Ma had cried, and Pa had gone around looking mad for a week. Then they'd seemed to forget all about Kirk until he came back.

"Well?" Matt prompted. "How about it, Kirk?"

"I don't think so," Kirk said finally.

They reached the yard and dismounted. Kirk said, "Put the horses up, Matt. Billy's got to eat. I doubt if he's had anything all day."

"No," Billy said. "I haven't." He had forgotten how hungry he was until just now.

He strode beside Kirk to the house. The big front room seemed almost bare now with the supplies and machinery moved out, and just a few pieces of furniture scrounged from other rooms in it. Kate came out of Guy's bedroom on the main floor. Her big face, hard touched by grief, showed instant relief when she saw Billy.

She came to him and hugged him, tears of relief running down her cheeks. Kirk said, "He's been riding all day. He was afraid to come home. He's pretty hungry, Kate."

"Why, sure he is, bless his heart. Come on, boy, I'll fix you something. Then you're going to bed. You look wore out."

She jerked her head toward the bedroom. Kirk asked, "No better?"

"No," Kate said. "No change at all."

Kirk walked slowly into the bedroom and stood looking down at his father. Guy's eyes were open, his lips parted. It seemed to Kirk he had never seen his father's face as pale as it was now. It was almost the color of wax.

He felt pity for Guy, even knowing he had brought this on himself. There was no sorrier sight than seeing his father's great body lying motionless and helpless, with only his eyes alive, eyes that glared at Kirk as though blaming him for what had happened.

"How are you, Pa?" Kirk knew at once that it was a foolish thing to say, so he added quickly, "I'm sorry this happened."

He thought he caught a bare movement of Guy's lips, but no sound came from them. He stepped back to the fringe of light and sat down, thinking of Eli Yockey and Luke Bartram and the rest of the Salt Creek bunch. They'd become bold, now that Guy was helpless, driven by desperation at the increasing gravity of their situation.

Kirk realized that his own bunch of cattle was no better off than Eli's and those of the others. His meager start would be destroyed along with the rest.

Presently Kate appeared in the doorway and motioned for him to come into the front room. He had known this was coming and he could guess what Kate was going to say. He left the bedroom and sat down on a straight-backed couch covered with two worn Navajo blankets. It was the least uncomfortable seat in the room.

Kate stood in front of him, her big legs spread, her hands on her hips. She said, "I reckon you know what this means."

He didn't reply. She went on, "It means he's helpless and dependent. It's a good thing I'm strong because he's no lightweight. I thought for a while today I'd never get him home. I had to come back and harness a team and take a wagon. I had to lift him into the wagon and carry him into the house when I got here. How I did it I'll never know."

He rolled a cigarette and lighted it, wishing she'd get to the point.

She cleared her throat. "Billy's fed and in bed. I got the story out of him, but I'd pretty well guessed what had happened because I found his fishing pole there beside Guy." Nervously she cleared her throat again. "Are you going to stay here and run Tomahawk, or are you going back to that Salt Creek bunch and let a good ranch go to the dogs?"

He looked at her, taking a long drag on his cigarette. "How long's he going to be like this?"

"Rest of his life, maybe. Sometimes they get better. Might even get so he can walk a little. But you haven't answered my question! And before you do, think a little on what you owe Tomahawk and your brothers and your Ma's memory . . ."

"I'm getting damned tired of hearing about what I owe," he said rebelliously, and rose and started toward the door.

Kate caught his arm. "Don't get ringy now. You've got a chance, one you never had before. You can make a better place out of Tomahawk than it was with Guy running it."

Kirk stood looking at her, not wanting to argue. Her eyes sparked with anger. "Tell me this. When the Salt Creekers move in, which they sure as hell will, where are you going to stand?"

Kirk frowned, remembering the way Guy had glared at him in the bedroom. This seemed to Kate and probably to everyone else a simple decision to make. But it wasn't—not after what had happened between him and Guy and what would certainly happen again if Guy ever got back on his feet.

He took Kate's hand firmly from his arm. How could he tell her what he was going to do when he didn't know himself?

Thirteen

Kirk smoked a cigarette, standing in front of the house, unaware of the cold wind that rushed down the valley of Beaver Creek, his mind too busy with his thoughts to give cognizance to personal discomfort. He finished the cigarette, frowning, then ground it out under his toe. When he went back in, he saw that Kate was gone. He supposed she was sitting beside Guy's bed.

He climbed the stairs to his room, discovering that Kate had kept it exactly as it had been when he'd left. He remembered how it had been the afternoon of his mother's funeral, how he'd stood here staring around the room and thinking he'd probably never see it again.

He thought about Billy, riding around frantically all day, caught in a squeeze between justifiable fear of his father on the one hand and helplessness on the other. It pleased him that Billy had thought of him as the only one to whom he could turn.

In a way, Kirk was caught in a similar squeeze. He felt keenly the obligation Kate talked about, one that had been hammered home earlier by Billy's turning to him. On the other hand there was his own long standing antagonism toward his father, an antagonism that Guy returned.

He guessed that in the final analysis, it boiled down to Guy's condition and his chances of recovery. Kirk didn't want to come back and then have to break with his father and leave all over again. Maybe he had too much pride, he thought ruefully. Maybe, as Kate had once said, he'd been born with this streak of rebellion in him. But that was the way he was made, and he couldn't help it any more than Guy could help doing the things he'd done.

He thought about Bianca. Maybe she could help him. He could talk to her, and would, in the morning. She'd understand his problem in a way that neither Kate nor anyone else would. He blew out the lamp and got into bed, wondering why he'd thought of Bianca instead of Rachel.

When he went downstairs in the morning, he found Doc Peters sitting at the kitchen table drinking a cup of coffee. He said, "Mornin', Doc—Kate."

"Howdy, Kirk," Peters said.

Kate, standing at the range frying bacon, asked, "Sleep all right, darlin'?"

He grinned. "Save your blarney for Guy." He drew back a chair and sat down. Kate was tired, he saw. He wondered how long even her great strength would stand up under the burden she had assumed. He looked at Doc. "What do you make of Pa?"

"I can't tell you much more than Kate did. Guy's had a bad stroke. I've warned him more than once, but he wouldn't listen. Now it's too late. There's very little I can do for him."

"Will he get better?"

Peters shrugged and took the platter of bacon from Kate. "Maybe. He's strong as a bull. I've seen men with a partial paralysis get over it. With Guy, I'd say the best you could expect would be that he'll hobble around on a cane. He'll be thick-lipped, but chances are he'll be able to talk some. He won't be able to express himself adequately, and that'll be hard on him. Knowing he brought it on himself won't be much help."

"No," Kirk said, thinking that Guy had always found it necessary to blame someone else for his own mistakes. He helped himself to the bacon, then asked, "It's not possible that he'll ever be like he was?"

The doctor shrugged. "I'm a doctor, not a prophet. But I think I can say he'll never be like he was. And I doubt very much that he'll ever take over running the ranch again, if that's what's bothering you." He gave Kirk a sharp look and then, unexpectedly, he grinned. "Now I've got to reverse myself. Your father's got a will like iron, and anything's possible for a man like that."

Kirk left the house as soon as he finished breakfast. He saddled and rode out, heading for the Chavez place. Doc Peters hadn't helped much. He certainly hadn't told Kirk what he needed to know.

Kirk wished he had more time, but he knew the time he did have was going fast. The Salt Creek bunch had a need too great to permit of waiting. If Guy had only leased the grass to them in the first place, this situation could have been avoided. Now it might be too late for a peaceful settlement.

Old and bitter hatred had smoldered for years between the Salt Creek ranchers and Tomahawk. They hated everything and everyone connected with it, and Guy had wantonly fanned their hatred into flame this year by his refusal to lease any grass. Kirk had seen the danger of their hatred and he understood it in a way that Guy would never understand it.

He reached the Chavez cabin and found Bianca in the back yard hanging up clothes. He reined up, asking, "Delfino here, Bee?"

"No, he's not," Bianca said tartly, "but I am. You can come in if you want to."

Kirk grinned as he stepped down. He left his reins dragging. Bianca's temper was a ready thing, always near the surface. As he went into the cabin, he wondered why he'd asked for Delfino. Bianca was the one he'd come to see.

She busied herself at the stove as Kirk dropped into a chair, keeping her back to him. The morning sunlight streamed through the window, bringing out the auburn highlights in her hair. When she poured a cup of coffee and brought it to him, he saw that color was high in her cheeks.

He said, "Sit down. I want to talk to you."

"I'm Bianca. Remember? You asked for. . . ."

"You'll do." He grinned. "Sit down."

She obeyed, her hands clasped tightly on her lap. He told her about Billy and what had happened to Guy. When he finished, she said, "I guess I'm just plain mean, but I can't waste tears on your father." She hesitated, watching him. "What are you going to do?"

"I haven't decided. I guess that's why I rode over here."

"To see Delfino?"

"No, to see you. Look . . ."

She broke in, her tone sharp, "You know what you're going to do, all right. You just want me to tell you you're doing the right thing."

He was irritated, both by her tone and her apparent lack of understanding. He said with equal sharpness, "All right, suppose you tell me what I'm going to do."

"You're going to stay. You can't stand seeing Tomahawk go under and you know that's what will happen if you don't stay and stop it. Matt can't do the job. You know what that Salt Creek crowd will do as soon as they hear about Guy."

He drank his coffee, aware that he did know. Maybe pride wasn't important when you balanced it against Tomahawk and Matt and Billy. He tapped his fingers against the oilcloth covering on the table. He thought of the bitterness that must be in Guy to have to depend on a son he'd told never to come back. But maybe he wasn't depending on him. Maybe he was counting on Matt. If he was, his bitterness must be unbearable, knowing he hadn't trained Matt to deal with emergencies. But would his feeling be one of bitterness? Kirk shook his head, realizing that he had no idea what was going on inside his father's head.

Kirk looked at Bianca. "I've got my own outfit down on Salt Creek. I've got twenty-two cows and eighteen calves on

Buck Point right now. I've got a stake, Bianca. It's all my own. If I come back to Tomahawk, I'll lose it. That bunch down there will burn my house and I'd never see any of my cattle again."

She got up and flounced across the room to the stove. She filled the fire box with wood, and then turned to face him.

"You're such a fool," she said. "If you go back to Salt Creek, you won't be able to stay. You'll never be one of them because they won't let you. They've hated the Van Horns too long. They'll fight Tomahawk for grass because there's nothing else they can do." Hands on hips, she stared at him challengingly. "Do you think you can stay with them when you know you'll be shooting at Matt and Billy and Frank Surrency and the rest of the Tomahawk men?"

She clenched her small fists at her sides. "Oh, Kirk, you *are* a fool if you think you can ever stay on Salt Creek."

He rose and picked up his hat, irritated by her anger. Why should she feel so strongly about this? The fact that she was right irritated him, too.

He guessed he'd known all along what he had to do. He just hadn't wanted to. Maybe Kate's urging had made him defensive about it, but Bianca had stripped all pretense away. She hadn't talked about loyalties and obligations. She'd laid the facts on the line simply and directly, facts which he knew but which seemed different when she said them in plain words.

"I guess you're right," he said wearily. "I was a fool to think I could do anything else."

She came to him and laid her hands on her arms, her head tipped back, eyes filled with more tenderness than he had ever seen there before. "Kirk, I'm sorry I talked like that, but you never ran away from a fight in your life, and this is a fight. You know it as well as I do."

He nodded, grinning ruefully. "Yeah, I know it. The hell of it is, it's hard for me to give up what I've got down there. I've been kind of proud of that little K Bar outfit. It was the first thing I ever owned in my life and it's not as easy to give it up as you think."

Tenderness left her eyes to be replaced by anger, sparkling with the intensity of a quick summer storm. "It's that . . . that Rachel Yockey more than your place that you hate to leave, isn't it? How do men get to *be* such fools?"

Kirk began to smile at her fury, but the smile only further infuriated her. She snapped, "When are you going to marry her?"

"Oh, I don't know." He grinned at her. "I haven't decided yet."

There were tears in her eyes now threatening to run over onto her smooth cheeks. She brushed them away angrily with the back of her hand.

He said quickly, "Good-bye, Bee," knowing he'd better get away, ashamed of having teased her.

He mounted and rode back toward Tomahawk, filled with gratitude to her in spite of her temper; then he put her out of his mind and thought of Guy. Kate wouldn't like what he intended to do, but he had to bring things out into the open, stroke or no stroke.

Guy could understand what he had to say. He'd tell Guy he was going to run Tomahawk, with no interference. He'd deal with the Salt Creek bunch in the way that seemed best, then he'd ride off when Guy was able to manage things again. But until then, he'd run things his own way.

After Kirk had left the Chavez cabin, Bianca sat at the table and pounded it with her fists. She was so angry she was trembling. Was every man as stubborn as Kirk Van Horn? Was every man as blind? Didn't he know she'd loved him ever since she'd been a little girl?

She remembered the time Kirk had left five years ago. She had been a child then, but she'd cried all the same. She'd thought he was never coming back. For reassurance she'd formed the habit of riding to Tomahawk to see Mrs. Van Horn on one pretext or another, and she always managed to ask casually if Kirk had written lately.

She smiled a little, remembering. Kirk's mother had been so calmly sure that Kirk would return someday that Bianca had begun to believe it herself.

And darn him, he was back now. Why couldn't he see she'd grown up? He saw the change in Rachel Yockey, all right. But Rachel had made him see it, flaunting herself around in front of him the way she had. If that was what a woman had to do to make a man know she existed, Bianca could do it as well as Rachel.

Her anger mounted again, then the tears came, releasing the pressure that had built in her for weeks. She was still crying when Delfino rode into the yard and put his horse away. She heard him and dried her eyes. She built up the fire so the coffee would be hot.

When Delfino came in, he looked at her intently as though sensing what had happened. He asked, "Kirk been here?"

She nodded. Delfino came to her and put his thin, wire-strong arms around her. "Easy does it, kitten. You've got to give Kirk time. I told you once that patience catches wolves. Remember?"

"Patience!" She stamped a small, booted foot. "You think I can be patient forever? I'll come right out and ask him to marry me! I can give him anything Rachel Yockey can if I have to."

"And be sorry the rest of your life." Delfino shook his head reprovingly. "Kirk will come around."

"And while I'm waiting for him to come around, he'll marry that . . . that . . ."

Delfino grinned at her. "Ah, ah, ah! Don't say it. You ain't supposed to know that kind of words."

She had to grin back at him. He sat down at the table and asked, "What was Kirk doing here?"

"You haven't heard about Guy?" When he shook his head, she told him, adding, "Kirk couldn't seem to make up his mind about staying. I lost my temper with him. I told him he was a fool."

"Well, he's not," Delfino said gravely. "Mighty few men with Kirk's pride would even come back. It's a hard choice for a man to make between being independent and staying home under the old man's thumb. Kirk's mighty loyal to take what he has and still come back."

She was ashamed then. She went to Delfino and put her face against his chest. "I didn't give him what I should have, did I? What's the matter with me? Can't I do anything right?"

Delfino patted her shining head. "You just try too hard, but you'll learn."

She got up and brought him his coffee. He said soberly, "I was just up by the Buck Point fence. They've got to come through, kitten. They don't have any choice. When they hear about Guy . . ."

She knew he was trying to prepare her for what was sure to come. There would be a fight. Men would be hurt, perhaps some would be killed. Kirk might be one of these.

She knew then that she, not Kirk, had been the fool, but now it was too late. She might not see him again before the trouble started. She might not have another chance. Again the tears began to well up into her eyes.

Fourteen

There was no hilarity in the men who assembled at the Salt Creek schoolhouse at sundown, only a grim-faced seriousness. The light of the dying day was cold and gray as they arrived. Some came on horseback. Some drove buckboards. But all were afraid and angry. Tonight they faced a decision that none of them wanted to make, now that the time for it had arrived.

The one exception was Shorty Hough. His face showed eagerness. His eyes were bright, his lips taut and thin. He was like a wolf scenting game. He stood on the raised platform at the front of the schoolhouse, the blackboards at his back, lamplight shining in his face. He greeted each of the newcomers by name, his tone hearty.

Eli sat on a bench behind Shorty. Like the others, Eli had his back to the wall. Yet, in spite of this and his hatred for Tomahawk, he had no enthusiasm for the decision he knew they would make tonight.

But as Shorty talked, Eli's face grew less gloomy, less oppressed. He knew Shorty better than the others did. He was a hard worker, he had all the toughness and courage a man could have, and he had never given Rachel up. That was the reason, Eli knew, that his hatred for Kirk Van Horn had become a raw, festering sore. But in Eli's mind, the most important quality in Shorty was his loyalty to the 3Y. It was this, Eli thought, which had made Shorty Hough, a hired hand, the real leader of the Salt Creek ranchers, a position that Eli was willing to surrender simply because he was growing old and tired.

As Eli listened, there was something Shorty left unsaid which spoke eloquently to him. Shorty was contending they had to move in on Tomahawk and take their grass, but what he didn't say was that they would vacate Tomahawk once the drought was over. The idea opened new vistas to Eli. The 3Y could be as big as Tomahawk. Perhaps in time he would own Tomahawk itself, regaining what he had once lost because Guy Van Horn had been the stronger man. Now Eli's eyes brightened, and he leaned forward, paying close attention to everything Shorty said.

"The old man's helpless," Shorty argued. "He's had a stroke and I hear he can't even talk. Matt and Billy are nothin'. The only thing we got to decide is what Kirk will do."

"What do you think he'll do?" Lew Warren demanded.

"Not a damned thing," Shorty answered with the grim certainty that characterized him these days. "By the time he gets wind of what we've done, we'll have cattle strung from one end of Tomahawk range to the other."

Chet Tappan, in the front row of benches, stood up. He had been one of the first settlers, a tall, slender man with a patient face. "You're talkin' a steal, Shorty. You're talkin' like you didn't mean to pay for that grass."

Shorty teetered back on his heels, a thick stump of a man who seemed as immovable as Cathedral Rim itself. "Chet, they tell me that years ago Guy pushed you down on Buck Point. Did he pay you for the grass he stole?"

This was a sore point with Eli and Tappan and several of the others, and Tappan's face turned red. Still he persisted, "I don't like it. Kirk's reasonable. I say we ought to ask him for the grass again, now that he's roddin' Tomahawk. I think we ought to pay two-bits a head like we agreed."

There was a rumble of argumentative voices in the room. Rachel, sitting beside Eli on the platform, looked down at the faces of the assembled men. Uneasiness grew in her as she listened to Shorty. She envisioned the Salt Creek men moving in on Tomahawk and led by Shorty. She understood him better even than Eli did, and so she was certain that Shorty had no intention of ever pulling off the plateau. That would ruin the plans she had nurtured for so long. She couldn't allow it to happen.

Rachel turned her head to look at her father, and saw in

him the same eagerness that was in Shorty. They were both fools, she thought angrily. Tomahawk had a large crew of hard-riding men. The Van Horns had a fortune in the bank. The law was on their side. They were bound to win. Her mind cried out, *No, there's a better way.*

She rose, startled by her own temerity. "Wait! You're letting Shorty stampede you into something foolish that will get some of you killed. All you want is grass. All right, Kirk will give it to you if you give him a chance to. Why kick up a war to get something you can have for the asking?"

Shorty wheeled on her, so infuriated by her interruption that for a time he was speechless. She smiled at him, not wanting to quarrel here in front of everyone, but she knew this was a course to which he would never agree because it left him out in the cold.

She cried, "Let me go to Tomahawk! I'll bring Kirk here to talk to you. Give him a chance to let you have the grass you need."

"That's reasonable," Tappan said. "What the hell can we lose?"

"Lose?" Shorty bellowed. "The advantage of surprise, that's what we'll lose!"

Rachel waited until the shouting voices died down, then she said, "You've lost that already. I won't stand here doing nothing while you sneak into Tomahawk's back door. I'm going to see Kirk tonight."

Shorty glowered at her. She saw in his eyes the will to strike her and suddenly she was afraid of him. He had changed in the months since Kirk had moved onto the K Bar. At first she had thought it was simply a matter of jealousy. Now, looking at his great, bull-like body and meeting his angry gaze, she knew that this had gone far past mere jealousy. It had become a matter of personal pride with Shorty, so personal and so bitter that he would not be satisfied until Kirk was dead.

Suddenly he wheeled away from her. For the moment at least she had won. She heard the murmur of approval from the crowd. She said. "I'll start right now." She couldn't wait until morning because she knew what would happen if she did. Shorty and Luke Bartram and some of the others would be on top of the mountain moving cattle toward the Toma-

92

hawk fence. She added, "I'll be back with Kirk by sunup. Why don't you go home and meet here first thing in the morning?"

Chet Tappan and Lew Warren and most of the others seemed relieved. They rose and began to leave the school-house. Shorty followed, trying without success to change their minds and growing steadily angrier.

Rachel turned to Eli. She said, "I'm going to marry Kirk, Dad. I'm going to live at Tomahawk. Can't you see how that changes things? Stealing range from Tomahawk is like steal-ing it from me."

Eli looked at her with interest. "Has he asked you? Or is he just playin' around with you like he did with Marge at the dance?"

"Who told you that?"

"Shorty."

"Shorty's a fool. Kirk just danced with Marge. That's all."

She caught a hint of the insecurity in Eli and was sur-prised by it. Then she realized she should have known. The shoe polish he used on his hair gave him away. He was afraid—terribly afraid he couldn't hold his young wife. She saw he didn't believe her statement that Kirk had made no play for Marge at the dance. Yet she also saw how much her talk of marrying Kirk relieved his mind.

Eli asked again, "Has he asked you?"

"No, but he will. There's always ways for a girl to get a man, if she wants him as bad as I want Kirk. I've got to go, Dad. Don't let Shorty do anything foolish."

"I'll try," Eli said heavily.

Shorty had turned at the door, calling angrily, "Rachel, you know you can't trust a Van Horn!" She deliberately avoided him by going out the side door. She ran across the yard and mounted her horse, glad now that they hadn't come in the buckboard as her father had first suggested.

She raced out of the schoolyard, ignoring Shorty's second warning about not trusting Kirk. As she rode, she made her plans, little tremors of excitement running through her body. She had failed the time she'd asked when they were getting married. This time it would be different.

She took the Tomahawk trail, wanting to negotiate it be-fore full dark blackened the land, but knowing it was impossible. At least she'd get above the cedars and onto the trail proper before dark, she thought. After that her horse would find the trail.

It was a long, hard ride to make at night, and it was after ten o'clock before she pulled up in the yard at Tomahawk. There was still a light in the living room, so she knocked at the front door.

Kirk answered it, his face showing his surprise when he saw her. "Come in, Rachel. Come in."

"Kirk, I'm sorry about Guy. Awfully sorry. How is he?"

He hesitated, watching her closely. Then he said, "Pretty good. He can't talk, but he's getting better. Doc says he may eventually get back on his feet."

Rachel glanced away, fighting to keep her composure. If Guy recovered, she'd be right back where she'd started. Tomahawk would be as remote as it had been before. She wondered how wise her present action was. But she was into it now. Maybe the doctor was wrong about Guy, anyway.

She looked up at Kirk, her emotions hidden behind the mask of urgency she wanted him to see. "Kirk, you've got to go back with me. Tonight! They had a meeting in the school-house and Shorty tried to talk them into moving in on you. I stopped it by telling them you'd probably give them the range they needed if they'd ask you. They're going to meet again first thing in the morning, but if you're not there, there's going to be trouble."

Kirk showed no hesitation and no doubt. He said, "Wait till I get my coat."

He disappeared into the back of the house and appeared a moment later wearing his sheepskin. He blew out the lamp and said, "Let's go. Everybody else is in bed. I was going over some of Guy's records. He's been pretty careless about things like that."

Rachel went out through the door and Kirk followed, closing it behind him. She waited while he caught and saddled a horse. Then she followed as he led out.

Her doubts steadily increased as she rode. She could still fancy herself married to Kirk, but her dream of living at Tomahawk began to fade. If Guy recovered, Kirk would return to his shack on the K Bar and Rachel would be worse off than she was now, living at home. She'd be better off

94

married to Shorty, she thought glumly. But it wouldn't be that way, she told herself. Guy wouldn't recover, she'd marry Kirk, and then she'd be mistress of Tomahawk.

Riding along with Rachel behind him, Kirk's mind was not on the girl. He was thinking ahead to the decision he must make. He had to decide what he was going to do before they reached the Salt Creek schoolhouse at dawn, but, like so many of the other decisions he had been forced to make lately, this was not an easy one.

If he leased the range as he had been inclined to do from the first, he would, in a sense, betray Guy. On the other hand, to refuse might also be a betrayal, for he understood the frame of mind into which the drought had forced the Salt Creek men.

He scowled into the darkness ahead. Life had a way of forever putting a man into an impossible situation where he was damned if he did, equally damned if he didn't. And that was exactly where Kirk would be when he faced the Salt Creek ranchers.

Well, he'd talk to them. He knew them and they knew him. Some, Chet Tappan and Lew Warren and a few others, were men that he trusted, but there was the other faction, Shorty Hough and Luke Bartram and their friends, men who couldn't be trusted no matter what agreement they made. And Eli? He wasn't sure. A few weeks ago he would have counted on him, but not now. It wasn't that he had anything definite to go on. It was just that Shorty Hough seemed to have the bit in his teeth and Eli was letting him run with it.

It would be the height of folly to precipitate a range war over grass that Tomahawk didn't need. Yet, if Guy learned what Kirk had done and had a relapse because of it, Kirk knew he would forever feel responsible.

Still undecided, he traveled this way, with Rachel close behind him. They passed the Chavez cabin and went on. They stopped at the cow camp and Kirk built a fire and made coffee. Rachel drank hers huddled in her coat, her shoulder pressed against Kirk. She seemed busy with her thoughts, so he didn't try to make conversation, but the mere pressure of her body against his stirred him in a way no other woman

95

ever had. She had one thing to give a man, and she never failed to make him aware of it when she was with him.

He started to kill the fire, but stopped when she said, "Come here, Kirk. We don't want to get there too early."

She sat on the edge of the bunk. As he walked toward her, she took off her coat and patted the bunk beside her. "Get me warm, Kirk. I got so chilled riding that I'm cold all the way through."

He sat down beside her and she leaned against him, shivering. He said, "I'll build up the fire. The cabin's tight enough. It won't take long to warm up."

"No, it's you I need, Kirk. It's not really the cold. I'm scared of what's going to happen. I can't bear to think of you being killed. Or badly hurt."

He put an arm around her. "I can take care of myself, so quit worrying. Besides, if I let them have the grass, there won't be any reason for anything to happen."

"No reason," she agreed, "but I know Shorty."

Her face was upturned to his, her red lips inviting. He tipped his head toward her and her lips met his. It was a woman's kiss, a hungry, passionate kiss that made his blood pound in his veins, a kiss that told him she wanted him as much as he wanted her.

Now, as she pulled his arm away from her and lay back on the bunk, he realized how much he had wanted her from the moment he had come back and found her a woman grown, full-bodied and desirable.

He lay down beside her, propping himself on one elbow so he could look at her, but she wouldn't have it that way. She reached up and brought him down beside her, whispering, "Kirk, I love you so much."

He was on his side, and now she turned so that she faced him, letting her body press against him. Pulse-pounding excitement mounted in him as he began tentatively to explore her soft, yielding body. She moaned; her eager mouth sought his, and he kissed her again.

When she drew her lips away from his, she said in a tone so low he would not have heard if her mouth had not been close to his ear, "I wouldn't let you do this before we're married, Kirk, if you weren't being so wonderful to us."

"Wonderful?" He propped himself up on an elbow again. "What do you mean by that?"

"Letting us have the grass. Guy wouldn't have done it. I don't suppose your brothers would, either."

She reached up to draw him down to her again, but his hunger for her had cooled as suddenly as if she'd doushed him with cold water. He sat up, disappointed and bitter, thinking that if a man took a woman, it should be when she wanted him, too, not to pay for a deal that would save her father's cattle, or to make certain he'd make such a deal.

"I see," he said, and got up.

"Kirk, what's the matter?"

He shook his head, looking down at her. He felt pity for her. "You don't know what's the matter?" he asked. "You honestly don't know?"

"Of course I don't," she cried.

"You were going to pay me for being a good boy," he said. "I give the Salt Creekers grass, so you reward me. You've got things a little wrong, Rachel. I'll do what I think is best for all concerned, not because you're willing to . . ."

"Kirk, it wasn't that way!" She sat up, confused and hurt. "I told you I loved you. I wanted you, and I hoped you wanted me."

But there was nothing now that she could say that would reach him. She had made a mistake, and all she could do was to make the best of it. She hadn't lied when she had told him she loved him. Compared to him, Shorty was nothing. She had wanted Kirk as well as Tomahawk that he'd bring to her; she had wanted a man of whom she could be proud, a Van Horn who would give her his name and his wealth.

She'd have to let him have more time. Maybe if she was very careful . . .

"We'd better ride," he said.

For a moment she sat there staring at his bleak face, and suddenly she realized that more time wouldn't change anything. She had lost him because she'd said the wrong thing. Or he'd taken it the wrong way. She hadn't really said it, she assured herself. It was just the perverse twist he had given her words.

He turned to the door. Suddenly a wave of anger rose

within her, and she cried, "You'll be sorry for this, Kirk!" She flung the words at him and rose and flounced out of the cabin.

He blew out the lamp, closed the door, and followed her to the horses. Mounting, they took the Salt Creek trail. As they dropped over the rim, the eastern sky turned gray with dawn. By the time they reached the bottom, the sun was staining the tips of the hills with scarlet and gold.

The schoolhouse was empty and cold when they went in. Kirk immediately built a fire in the pot-bellied stove. Rachel had said nothing all the way down from the rim. Now she huddled in front of the stove, her hands held out, shivering, her face bitter with her thoughts.

Whatever had once been between them was gone and Kirk had no regrets. He had his own problem, one he had wrestled with for hours, and after pacing restlessly around the room, he reached a decision. He'd let them have the grass, but he'd make it clear it was only a temporary agreement because of the emergency.

Rachel had said she knew Shorty. Well, Kirk did, too. It would be like the man, along with Luke Bartram and the others who would side with him, to try and hold the range once they had it, but that wasn't anything to worry about. Tomahawk could and would move them off when the time came.

Eli and Shorty were the first to arrive. Shorty remained coldly aloof, saying nothing. Eli grunted a sour "Morning," in response to Kirk's greeting, then glumly sat down on a bench to wait, his big-knuckled hands on his knees.

Rachel stirred, her eyes on Shorty, calculating, mentally measuring him against Kirk. The sunlight crept down the cedar slopes and touched the bottom of the valley. Presently the rest of the Salt Creek men began to ride in, in ones and twos, and groups of three or four.

Even after a dozen or more had gathered in the schoolhouse, Eli remained on the bench, his hands still on his knees. Impatiently Rachel said, "Let's get started, Dad. They're waiting."

Eli got up, frowning. He glanced at Kirk, plainly showing that he hated to ask a Van Horn for anything. He cleared his throat, looking at Shorty uncertainly as if seeking direc-

98

tion. Kirk had never thought of Eli as an old man, but he showed his age now, and Kirk realized more than ever that Eli had abdicated his leadership in favor of Shorty Hough.

Eli cleared his throat again, glancing at Shorty a second time. Shorty had sat down in the first row, confident and apparently pleased with himself.

"You know the grass situation, Kirk," Eli said haltingly. "We figure with your pa sick, you'd be the one to make a deal with us."

Eli sat down without waiting for Kirk to answer. Now, as Kirk rose and faced the crowd, he noticed that the men were divided into two factions, Shorty's bunch, on the left, the others on the right. Kirk was silent for a moment, his gaze moving from Shorty's face to Luke Bartram's and on to the rest of the men who sat behind Shorty, and it struck him that these men actually wanted him to refuse. With that thought came the conviction that he had wasted his time coming here.

"I know the grass situation, all right," Kirk said. "And I'm willing to let you have grass at two bits a head, but get one thing straight. *This is for the emergency only . . .*"

A sound that was almost an animal growl came from Shorty's throat. He jumped to his feet, yelling intemperately, "We won't pay you a cent! Your old man drove us off the plateau, and now by God, we're takin' it back!"

"Hold on, Shorty," Eli said, but there was no controlling the man.

Shorty wheeled to face the others. "What you waitin' for? Get movin'! Get up there on Buck Point and cut the fence. Start drivin' cattle onto Tomahawk grass. By sundown it won't *be* Tomahawk grass! It's ours by rights, so let's take it!"

"You gone loco, Shorty?" Lew Warren was on his feet, his face pale. "Kirk's giving us the deal we wanted. What's the use of fighting over something we've just had give to us?"

"He don't aim to 'give' us nothing!" Shorty shouted. "I ain't the one that's loco, and I ain't yellow, neither!"

"Don't call me yellow!" Warren yelled.

Eli pounded the desk. "Lew! Shorty! This ain't getting us nowhere! Let's have order . . ."

99

But none of the Salt Creekers was listening to Eli. Shorty and Luke Bartram and their bunch were on their feet facing Lew Warren and his group, standing on the other side of the aisle. Kirk, watching, saw the whole thing had gotten out of hand and that Eli was completely helpless. If the Salt Creekers were going to fight among themselves, he'd go home and let them have at it.

He turned toward the side door, wondering why he had ever let Rachel talk him into coming, then stopped and swung back, for he heard Shorty's voice booming above the others, "It's time we learned the Van Horns they can't have everything just because they're Van Horns. We can't trust Kirk any more than we could trust his old man."

Rachel had been sitting beside the stove, watching and listening. After she had left the line cabin with Kirk she had been too numb to think straight, but by now she was mentally alert. She'd had time to consider what happened in the cabin, how close she had come to putting her brand on Kirk for good and all. She had supposed she'd said the wrong thing, but now, looking back, she doubted that she had. There was a better explanation for Kirk's sudden reversal of attitude. Bianca Chavez was on his mind, and something must have reminded him of her.

For a time Rachel had let her thoughts dwell with hate on Bianca, but she realized presently that was accomplishing nothing. Kirk Van Horn was the one to be hated. She wanted him brought down and destroyed; she wanted him beaten and torn apart until he begged her to save him.

Now, watching Shorty and listening to him, she suddenly saw that he was a man and she could use him. He had strength and cold-blooded courage. He was proving that by his bold bid for leadership, and all at once she knew how she could bring Kirk down and set Shorty up as the leader of the Salt Creekers. She would have to pay a price, but it would be worth it.

She ran to the front of the room. Lew Warren was yelling something at Shorty, and Eli, confused and impotent, was vainly trying to restore order. She waved her arms to attract their attention, but she failed until she noticed the bell on the desk. She picked it up and rang it. Slowly the shouting died

100

as they turned to her and heard her cry, "Listen to me! Listen!"

Shorty's big hand waved his group into silence as he said harshly, "I don't know what the hell she wants to say, but I'd rather listen to her than Lew Warren."

She was very pale and her lips were quivering. Kirk had no idea what she was going to say, but he couldn't keep from feeling sympathy for her. She looked in this moment like a woebegone, friendless child.

Rachel didn't try to speak until the silence was complete. Then she said in a voice that barely reached the men in front of her, "I guess I know Kirk Van Horn better than any of you. Lew and some of the rest of you seem to think you can trust him, but you can't. He's *worse* than Guy. I'm ashamed to tell you, but of all people I ought to know."

Staring at her, Kirk could not believe what he was hearing, then he remembered her telling him he'd be sorry. Suddenly he knew what she was going to say before she said it, and he knew equally well that any denial he made would not be believed.

"The worst of it is that I believed his promises," she hurried on. "Tonight I begged him to marry me, but he laughed at me. What did he care that I'd been fool enough to believe him? He's a Van Horn! I'm just a Salt Creeker, not good enough for him. He . . . took his pleasure, and that was all he wanted."

"You're not telling the truth!" Kirk shouted. "Tell them . . ."

"I'm telling the truth, all right!" She whirled to face him. "I suppose you've forgotten what happened that night coming down off the rim. But I haven't, and I never will. You ought to be ashamed of yourself, and you ought to be more than ashamed for refusing to marry me when I begged you tonight."

The Salt Creek men had been listening open-mouthed, not quite believing Rachel's story. Shorty yelled, "Now he calls her a liar! By God, let's hang him for what he done to her!"

That was all it took to change them into a blood-lusting mob. They'd hang him, Kirk knew, if he stood here and let them do it. In a matter of seconds the anger they had been venting on each other was turned against him. That was ex-

101

actly what Rachel had sought, and she had succeeded, at the cost of her good name.

Eli grabbed Kirk's arm, his face contorted by agony. Kirk jerked loose as the crowd rushed him, Shorty in the lead. Kirk hooked a chair with his boot toe and kicked it directly at Shorty. It crashed into his face before his gun was leveled, giving Kirk the brief instant of time that he needed. He yanked his gun from its holster and put a shot over the men's heads, stopping their forward movement.

"Hold it," he said. "Nobody's hanging me. You want to believe Rachel, so you will, but she's lying and Shorty picked up her lie."

Cowed by his gun, they remained motionless as he moved to the side door. He put his hand on the knob and opened it. He said, "The first man who comes through here will get shot."

He was grateful that there were no windows on this, the north side of the building. Stepping quickly through the door, he slammed it shut behind him, and ran across the yard. He reached his horse as the door was flung open. He threw a quick shot at the schoolhouse and heard the bullet thud into the log wall. He untied his horse and swung onto its back. He reined around and spurred into the tall sagebrush, crouching low over the horse's neck.

A rifle barked behind him. The slug ricocheted from a rock nearby and whined off into the darkness. Kirk heard shouting voices behind him and a volley of shots that sounded like a string of firecrackers.

Then he turned into a ravine and was clear. But time was short. He doubted if he could get to Tomahawk and return before the Salt Creek bunch cut the fence and pushed their cattle onto Tomahawk range. He dug in his spurs and the horse mounted the steep slope in frantic, urgent lunges.

It was war now. Nothing could stop it. They'd believed Rachel's lie, so they'd be doing more than fighting for grass. They'd be avenging a woman who'd been betrayed. Yet Kirk wasn't sure that Rachel's lie was as important as it had seemed a moment ago. Sooner or later Shorty would have beaten down the weaker ones. If it hadn't been Rachel's lie that Shorty had used to unite the Salt Creekers, it would have

102

been something else. They had nursed their hatred of Guy Van Horn too long. Now, because of it, Tomahawk would be fighting for its life.

Fifteen

Kirk put his horse up the steep trail at a speed he had not thought possible, yet he was careful to stop and allow the horse to blow whenever he reached a spot hidden from the trail below. He could see the Salt Creek men coming far below him like a file of ants.

He was four or five hundred yards above them, beyond the effective range of a rifle, yet now and then he would hear the flat bark of a Winchester, or see a spurt of dust kicked up from the talus slope beneath him by a bullet. He was appalled at what had happened, and he realized with a shock that they were actually trying to kill him.

He was able to maintain his lead gained at the cost of the virtual exhaustion of his horse. He was gambling on the chance that he'd be able to rope a loose horse once he reached the top of the plateau. If he failed in this . . . He shook his head worriedly.

He reached the top and spurred up the steep slope above the rimrock until he reached the rolling ground of the plateau proper. From here he scanned the land ahead, looking frantically for the dark shapes of grazing horses. He saw cattle, but no horses.

With a sinking heart, he angled down a ridge in the direction of Tomahawk's cow camp, still holding his exhausted horse to a canter. The animal's neck was covered with froth. His breathing was hoarse and uneven. Now and then he faltered and almost fell.

Reluctantly Kirk reined to a halt. He had to rest his mount or the animal would not have the strength to run down a loose horse if and when he found one.

Kirk dismounted hastily and yanked the saddle from the animal's back. He pulled off the sodden saddle blanket and fanned the horse with it. After a couple of minutes he flung the blanket and saddle back on and cinched up. He mounted and rode out, hunting cover in the high brush and sparse timber.

He traveled this way for another ten minutes, and then, unexpectedly, crested a low rise and saw a group of grazing horses before him. Scarcely breathing, he took down his rope. He eased his mount toward the bunch, praying they wouldn't spook away until he got close.

They didn't. When he was ten yards from the nearest one, a white-stockinged bay, he reined over and flipped out his loop. It settled neatly over the startled horse's head. Kirk dallied immediately. The horse lunged away, but when he felt the rope tighten, he stopped and stood, trembling.

Kirk unsaddled and released his horse. Then he threw down his saddle and bridle, and went hand over hand along the rope until he reached the bay and led him back. The animal tried to avoid the bridle, but Kirk forced it on. He saddled and tightened the cinch just in time. Half a dozen Salt Creek men came over the rise behind him, raising a shout when they saw him.

Kirk swung astride, coiling his trailing rope as the bay bunched beneath him. The horse wanted to buck, but Kirk held his head up with a determined hand and touched his sides with the spurs. The bay lunged out.

A rifle barked behind Kirk, but this time he only grinned. The horses of his pursuers were spent. His was fresh. And after that shot it would be impossible for them to catch fresh horses for themselves out of the bunch that had galloped away.

In mid-morning Kirk drew his lathered, plunging horse to a stop before the Chavez cabin, calling, "Delfino! You home?"

The door opened and Delfino appeared with Bianca behind him. Thank God he hadn't been off somewhere hunting wolves!

Kirk said, "They're going to cut the Buck Point fence and drive their stock onto Tomahawk range! Know where you can find some of our crew fast?"

Delfino nodded. Kirk looked down at Bianca. She said, "I thought you were going to let them have grass."

"I was, but they changed my mind." He decided not to

mention the part Rachel had played in the trouble. "Now that Guy's laid up, they've got the notion they can have Tomahawk grass free."

"What are you going to do?"

He grinned with cool assurance. "Stop them. We'll run 'em off Buck Point if we have to." He whirled and set his spurs, calling to Delfino who had gone into the cabin for his boots and now reappeared, "Bring all the men you can find back here. I'll meet you."

Delfino nodded and headed for the corral. Bianca stood in front of the cabin, looking small and frightened.

When Kirk reached Tomahawk, he found two men working in one of the fields. They had a hayrack loaded with hay. One man was driving and the other was pitching hay off to the blocky bulls that followed along behind the wagon. Kirk reined up, calling, "Head that rig for the yard. The Salt Creek bunch is moving in."

He rode on toward the house, hearing the rattling and squeaking of the hayrack behind him. Matt was working with Frank Surrency on the storehouse that Guy had ordered built after Kate made him clean out the living room. When they heard the news, they ran for the corral. Matt saddled and rode out to the horse pasture to bring in the horse herd.

Guy was sitting in the rocker on the porch. That was ironic, Kirk thought, for Kate had told him how Guy hated that damned chair. When Guy looked at him, Kirk said, "The Salt Creekers are moving in, but we can stop 'em if we move fast enough."

Guy tried to speak, but his lips only twitched. His eyes seemed to demand more details. Kate came to the door and looked questioningly at Kirk. Kirk said, for Kate's benefit as much as Guy's, "I'd decided to let 'em have the grass, but they figured they could take it for nothing. They were shooting at me when I left."

The hay wagon rolled into the yard and the men hastily unhitched. Billy was carrying two buckets of water from the creek. He put them down and ran to the front of the house in time to hear what Kirk had said. Kate's heavy, muscular arms were covered with soapsuds. Apparently she had been washing clothes and Billy was toting water for her.

"Can I go, Kirk?" Billy cried. "Please?"

105

Kirk shook his head. "You stay here and look after things."

Billy's face showed his disappointment. Surrency came from the corral leading three horses he had saddled. Matt rode up on his own mount. Kirk looked at the men, asking, "Got your guns and plenty of shells?"

They nodded. Kirk studied them. Their faces were calm, as if riding out to fight and perhaps get killed was all part of a day's work.

"We'll be outnumbered," Kirk said.

Nobody said anything. Their expressions didn't change. Kirk said, "Come on, then."

As he mounted, Kirk glanced at Guy. His eyes were troubled. Kirk thought he detected wistfulness in them. He wanted to go, Kirk knew. He had no faith in his sons. The knowledge shook Kirk's faith in himself. What if he failed?

They left the meadows and swept into the timber at a run. Taking the lead, Kirk headed for Delfino's cabin. He hoped the old wolfer was back. If he wasn't, they'd have to go on without him.

Kirk glanced behind. He had four men besides himself. And Shorty Hough was leading between fifteen and twenty Salt Creek men.

But Delfino was back, though he'd been able to find only one man, a new hand named Slim Nelson. The pair, mounted and ready, fell in behind Kirk and his bunch as they swept past the cabin.

Bianca stood in the doorway, a hand shading her eyes from the sun. She called worriedly, "Be careful. Be careful." Kirk acknowledged her words with a wave. Then they were out of the clearing and entering the timber again.

Kirk picked the shortest route, carefully measuring the horses' strength against their speed and the rate of climb. Several times he stopped; several times he slowed to a walk. They had to get there fast, but balanced against the need for haste was the fact that they couldn't afford to leave a man behind because a horse played out.

They reached the cow camp and went on. Now, angling left, Kirk saw the bare, rolling slopes of Buck Point ahead, and at the same time he saw the dark, red shapes of the Salt Creek cattle spreading out toward him like a shifting tide.

106

Kirk pulled up in a clump of scrub oak, motioning for the others to stop. Underfoot, last year's leaves were dry and crackling. Frank Surrency and the rest looked at him, waiting for his orders. Matt's face was white, his eyes dilated with fear.

"We've got a choice," Kirk said. "We take the men or we take the cattle. What do you think, Frank?"

Surrency would take no responsibility. He said, "You're the boss."

Kirk knew he was right. This was his first test, and he had to call this the way it should be called if he expected to fill Guy's boots. He winked deliberately at Matt and it seemed to buck his brother up. Matt's shoulders straightened. Kirk turned his gaze to Delfino, but the old wolfer's inscrutable expression gave him no help.

"We'll take the cattle first," Kirk said. "Maybe we won't have to take the men."

He saw approval in both Surrency's and Delfino's eyes. Kirk said, "All right then, spread out. Drive the cattle in front of you and drive them fast. If they want a fight, they'll get it, but put the cattle through the fence if you can."

They rode out, spreading like a fan. None of the cattle had entered the timber. The reason was plain enough. They were nearly starved. They were grazing as though they hadn't seen a blade of grass for a week, yanking it up in great mouthfuls.

They were hard to turn, hard to start moving. Kirk rode like a madman, firing his revolver, shouting, swinging a vicious, knotted rope-end at their scrawny rumps. He angled back and forth, and gradually got them moving.

He glanced around and saw that the others were doing the same. The herd was turned and headed back, but no one let up. Still they rode, yelling, whistling, swinging the knotted ends of their ropes. They emptied their guns and reloaded and emptied them again. Finally the cattle broke into a shambling run. The men reloaded and shoved their revolvers back into holsters.

The cattle approached the cut fence. A section almost a quarter of a mile long had been ripped out. The herd funneled through just as the Salt Creek bunch rode out of a draw on the rimrock side driving another bunch before them.

They dropped the bunch immediately when they saw the Tomahawk men. For an instant they sat their horses, unmoving, startled, not having believed it possible for Kirk to reach Tomahawk and return this soon.

"Come on," Kirk called, and set his spurs deep in his horse's sides. He thundered through the cut fence and straight down upon the Salt Creekers.

He was gambling on their surprise, and on something else. *They weren't ready for a shooting fight.* He yanked his horse to a stop not more than a yard from Shorty Hough, plunging and wild-eyed. His gun was still in his hand. Looking into Shorty's face, he knew the man was going to draw, for his face was livid, his eyes that of a man whose fury had carried him far beyond the point of reason.

Kirk didn't hesitate. His spurs gouged his horse's sides and the animal leaped ahead. Passing Shorty, Kirk's gun hand swept out, striking the man a hard blow on the side of the head. Then he was past and in the middle of the milling Salt Creek crowd. Shorty slid out of his saddle head first.

Kirk didn't stop. He went on through, and when he turned, his gun was steady in his hand. He said bleakly, "All right, who'll be first? Who's going to be first? Eli? Luke? Which one?"

The silence seemed to run on endlessly, a silence broken only by hoarse breathing and fidgeting horses. A grin tugged at the corners of Kirk's mouth. "All right, boys, take your cattle and get the hell out of here."

Lew Warren and Chet Tappan dismounted, and loading Shorty on his horse, tied him down. Luke Bartram leaned forward in his saddle, his sullen eyes on Kirk, but in the end Kirk stared him down. Tappan and Warren mounted, and the entire Salt Creek bunch rode away downcountry without a backward glance.

Sixteen

Kirk sat his saddle and watched the Salt Creek bunch until they dropped from sight into a long ravine. The sun was warm

108

this afternoon, and pleasant after so many days of cold and hazy skies.

He should have been elated at the victory he'd won, but no elation was in him. Instead, depression weighed upon him. If they had let him, he would have given the Salt Creekers what they needed, taking a chance on Guy's fury, but the way they had believed Shorty's lie and turned on him was proof of the long-time hatred they'd had for the Van Horns. It explained why they had never accepted him. And now, he would never be able to go back.

Shrugging, Kirk turned to Delfino and the Tomahawk crew. "Let's put the fence up," he said. "I don't think they'll try it again."

Delfino was watching him with his wise old eyes. He grunted, "Don't be too sure."

Kirk grinned at him. "You've been running with the wolves too long, Delfino. We're dealing with coyotes, not wolves."

They dismounted and began to untangle the barbed wires that had been ripped from the fence. Slim Nelson had been fixing fence when Delfino found him, so he had fencing tools on his saddle. Kirk cut his hand several times on the barbs, but within two hours they had the wires back up, spliced together, tightened, and stapled into place. This was a good, five-wire fence. It had to be to keep Salt Creek cattle from breaching it to get at the feed on the Tomahawk side.

Matt had been dogging Kirk's heels all afternoon, watching him with a near-worshipful expression that embarrassed Kirk. Once Matt said, "Boy, that was something to see! That was *sure* something, the way you made that bunch tuck their tails between their legs. Dad should've seen it."

Kirk turned and grinned at him. "Come on. Let's get back or Kate's good grub will be cold."

"Ain't you afraid they'll do it again?"

Kirk shook his head. "Not very likely. Shorty's going to have a hell of a headache when he wakes up. I'll send a couple of men up here in the morning to guard the fence."

He saw the gleam of an idea in Matt's eyes. Matt said, "I think somebody ought to stay tonight. Just in case."

Kirk swung into the saddle. The others were mounted and moving away. Matt remained on the ground, his face turning stubborn. Kirk stared down at him, thinking how much Matt looked like Guy Van Horn right now. There was a steadiness in his eyes, a firmness to his mouth that Kirk had never seen there before.

He said, "Kirk, I want to stay."

The others had ridden off a hundred yards and were waiting. Matt said desperately, "Kirk, the old man's kept me under his thumb all my life. He's never let me do a damned thing by myself. I'm a nothin', and I'm scared to stay here, but if I don't do it, I'll never amount to a damn. Can you see that?"

Kirk could see it. He could also see a possibility in this situation he hadn't admitted to anyone. He might be underestimating the Salt Creek men. They might try again. It was true that Shorty Hough would have a headache when he came to, but it was equally true that he'd be crazed by a wild fury that had been building in him for weeks.

But he realized, too, how important this thing had suddenly become to Matt.

"All right," he said finally, "if you'll promise to burn the trail for home if they try to cut the fence. Don't try to stop 'em. Just come running for help. One man couldn't stop them anyway. I wouldn't care who he was."

Matt nodded. His face was paler than before, and Kirk felt a moment's doubt. Matt was plainly scared. But if he stayed tonight he might lick that fear. . . .

"No need to stay all night," Kirk said. "If they don't show up by midnight, chances are they won't show at all. Come on home and get a little sleep." He nodded at his brother as he reined away. "Good luck, kid." He cantered to where Delfino and Frank Surrency and the rest of the crew were waiting. "Matt's going to stay on a while."

Worry crawled across Delfino's dark face. "I don't like it, Kirk."

"He promised to come for help if anything happened," Kirk said. "I told him not to stay after midnight."

He turned his head as he went over the rise. Matt had mounted and was heading up the ridge toward a spot that would overlook almost the entire length of the fence. Kirk was as worried as Delfino, but he understood Matt's need to stay. What happened during the next few hours would make Matt Van Horn, or ruin him.

The miles dropped behind. Delfino stopped off at his cabin. Kirk dismounted while the crew rode on. Delfino went inside. Bianca had come out and stood in the fading light looking up at Kirk's face. Her voice betrayed the agony of worry that was in her when she asked, "What happened?"

"Nothing much. We drove their cattle back through the break in the fence. Then we fixed it and came home."

"Didn't they try to stop you?"

He grinned. "They tried. I slugged Shorty and that was the end of it."

Her worry turned to anger. "Hmmm, just like that." When he didn't say anything, her face grew paler and her eyes flashed. "Kirk, you might have been killed!"

The intensity of her voice surprised him. He said, "Quit worrying, Bee, or you'll make an old woman out of yourself before it's time."

She glared at him for a moment, then whirled and fled into the cabin, slamming the door behind her savagely. Kirk looked after her in puzzlement. Now what had brought *that* on?

He rode across the clearing and into the timber, his worried thoughts returning to Matt. Maybe he'd been foolish to leave Matt up there. But what could happen? Matt had promised not to start anything by himself.

He felt a warm glow of respect for his brother. Matt had shown more courage this afternoon than he'd ever shown before in his life. Maybe it wasn't too late for him. Now that Guy was helpless, Matt might grow into the man he was capable of becoming. The thought cheered Kirk and he began to hurry, suddenly hungry for one of Kate's good suppers.

His splitting headache was the first thing Shorty Hough became conscious of. Blood had congested in it, and it throbbed with maddening, virulent intensity. Next, he was conscious of the horse's movement, which aggravated the headache. Full consciousness came with a rush, and along with it was a towering anger, anger at his failure to seize Tomahawk range and at the humiliating position in which he found himself.

He struggled to come upright, and failing, let out a furious

111

bellow, *"God damn it, cut me loose! What the hell. . . ?"*

The horse stopped. Luke Bartram and Eli hurried to him, cut him loose and eased him to the ground. Shorty got up. The men before him were blurred. He backed up to lean against a pine tree and pressed his hands to his head.

After a while, he looked around, realized where he was, and yelled, "What's goin' on? You give up?"

Eli shrugged. "What else could we do?"

Shorty looked at him sourly, hating this abject acceptance of defeat. He squinted at the sun, now hanging low in the west. He shook his head savagely, trying to clear it. He stared at them with scathing contempt. His voice was like acid.

"Yellow bellies! What'll you do now, go home and whine and wait for your cows to die? Or will you act like real men and *take* that damned grass for 'em?"

Only Luke Bartram had been able to meet his eyes. Now he whooped delightedly, "See? I told you what he'd say."

Eli cleared his throat. Shorty, recognizing the signs, swung on him fiercely. "It takes more'n shoe polish to make a young man out of an old one. Marge can tell you that, you old fool!"

He didn't know if the allusion would be understood by the others and he didn't care. He saw Eli's face go dull red, saw Eli's hand drop toward his gun as the large veins in his forehead began to throb. Shorty's sharp "Don't!" halted Eli's draw. He stood staring at Shorty, an old man painfully aware of his age. He was a beaten man, too, Shorty saw, and he'd go along because he no longer had the will to resist.

In a more reasonable tone, Shorty said, "We're wastin' time. Them cattle ain't far from the fence. Likely they're practically hangin' over it. Gather 'em up while me'n Eli and Luke cut the fence again."

His head still pounded, but his vision had cleared. He mounted his horse, hating the Van Horns with more virulence than he had ever hated anything. Especially, he hated Kirk, who was responsible both for the lump on his head and his ignominious defeat. For the loss of Rachel, too. Damn both of them! But he'd get her back. It would be different now.

The sun was down when they reached the fence, but its

112

red glow was on the sky and on the thin cloud layer that hung high above the Utah desert to the west. Shorty found his wire-cutters and, dismounting, quickly snipped all five wires. Then he handed one up to Eli.

"Dally that around your saddle horn," Shorty said, "and git movin'. We ain't got all night."

Eli looked at him as though wondering when things had changed, when he had stopped giving the orders and Shorty had begun. But he obeyed without speaking. Shorty handed the second wire up to Bartram, and Bartram took off with it. It creaked and squeaked, and the sound of staples popping out was shrill in the fading light.

Shorty started to grab the third wire himself when he sensed movement on the crest of a ridge on the Tomahawk side. He looked up. The shape of a man materialized about three hundred yards away. The man hesitated, rifle in his hands, then Shorty saw him throw the gun to his shoulder.

Sudden satisfaction was in Shorty. Damn the Van Horns! Damn them all to hell. Here was his chance to even a lot of scores.

He yanked his rifle from the saddle boot. He levered a shell into the chamber and threw it to his shoulder. Resting it carefully on the top of a fence post, he drew an exact bead on the distant man's chest.

It must be Kirk up there, Shorty thought. He was cold and steady, but his brain seethed with hate. He noticed that Kirk was hesitating. Then to Shorty's surprise, Kirk took the rifle from his shoulder and turned toward his horse.

Shorty followed him carefully with the sights. His mind told him, *Allow for the distance. Lead a little to allow for his movement.*

Carefully Shorty squeezed the trigger. Even before Kirk began to fall, Shorty knew he had scored a hit, for he heard the peculiar, indescribable sound of his bullet striking solid flesh.

The distant figure stopped, and bent over as though to pick something up. But he never straightened. Quietly, deliberately, he folded forward, and lay in a motionless heap.

Eli galloped back. "You killed him! You damn fool, you've fixed us now! What the hell did you do that for?" Eli's

113

voice rose until he was screaming. "You chuckle-headed son of a bitch, we're in for it now!"

Shorty looked up. "Wipe the spit off your chin, old man," he said. "What was I supposed to do, let him shoot me?"

"He wasn't aiming to shoot," Eli screeched. "He lowered his gun and turned away!"

"So he turned away," Shorty snarled, as much at the others who had ridden up as at Eli. "I suppose you wanted him to ride back to Tomahawk and fetch the whole pack of 'em down on us?"

Chet Tappan, his face gray and frightened, said, "But you didn't need to kill him. You could of . . ."

His voice trailed off. Shorty prompted, "I could of what?"

Tappan wiped his forehead with his shirt sleeve. "I'm gettin' the hell out of here."

A rumble of agreement rose from the others. Shorty silenced them with a gesture of his big hand. "Like hell you're gettin' out! We're all in this together. Every one of you is guilty—just as guilty as me. What the hell was we doin' just now? Stealin' range from Tomahawk, wasn't we? And who was we stealin' it for? Me? Hell no! We were stealin' it for you! In the eyes of the law that makes you guiltier'n me. Put that in your pipes and smoke it."

All the anger was gone from Eli Yockey's face. In its place was a sick hopelessness. He said wearily, "What do we do now, Shorty?"

"That's better, a lot better! You listen to me and we'll pull this off, but we won't get nothin' but a rope on our necks if you keep backin' out! I'll tell you what we'll do. We go home and keep our mouths shut. The cattle will drift through the fence durin' the night."

"Who was that you plugged?" Bartram asked.

"Kirk. Who else would be hangin' around?"

Lew Warren, as sick about this as Eli, asked, "What about him?"

Shorty scowled. He'd been panicked by the killing almost as much as the others, but he hadn't shown it. That was the trick, let them think he'd pull them through! He glanced at Eli, who had been telling him what to do all the months he'd worked for the 3Y. Suddenly he felt a great sense of satisfaction. Eli wasn't telling him anything now. Eli didn't see

where they were going to wind up, either. Only Shorty could
see that. As soon as he had this bunch lined out, so scared
they had to do what he told them, he'd run the rest of the
Van Horns out of the country.

"Ain't but one thing we can do," Shorty said. "Pitch his
body off the rim. Time they find him they won't know
whether he was shot or not."

Chet Tappan shuddered. Lew Warren's mouth was trembling at the corners. But Luke Bartram was grinning, as if
this was something to be enjoyed.

"Take your pick, boys," Shorty said savagely. "Pitch him
over or hang. Which is it goin' to be?"

Seventeen

Dusk had crept across the land as they talked. The thin
cloud layer to the west had faded and turned deep gray.

Shorty's words seemed to hang in the cooling air, a threat
over all of them. Luke Bartram, more subdued than usual,
asked, "You sure it was Kirk?"

Shorty said, "Yeah. Who else on Tomahawk would be
watchin' the fence, with Guy laid up? Now there's nothin'
standin' in our way. We can cut the pie any way we please."

He kicked the down wires aside so the others could ride
through. Then he mounted and followed, his lip curling at
the way they hung back. He forged ahead, calling impatiently, "Come on, come on! We ain't got all night."

The dry grass on the Tomahawk side rustled under their
feet. A small group of gaunt Salt Creek cattle approached
the break in the fence and cautiously picked their way
through, afterward breaking into a run as though the abun-
dance of feed had already strengthened them.

Shorty's contempt for the men behind him grew. Did they
think Guy Van Horn had built Tomahawk by pussyfooting
around and humbly asking for the things he wanted? Hell
no! He'd built it by acting just as Shorty had acted tonight,
decisively, ruthlessly.

In spite of the shock the killing had caused in him, Shorty

115

felt vastly proud of himself. He began building day dreams in which he saw himself using the 3Y to become the undisputed master of Tomahawk's enormous domain. Kirk Van Horn was dead, so Rachel would come back to him. That was the key to all his plans. Eli was a temporary front for him, but Eli wouldn't live much longer. Not that it made any difference. He could handle the old man. He'd already demonstrated that.

There would be no complications from the law. The trick was to prove to Red Henessy that the Salt Creekers were coming out on top. As long as Guy Van Horn had run Tomahawk, the sheriff had been his man, but Guy wasn't running Tomahawk now, and Henessy wasn't a man to back a loser.

Shorty had no great respect for the law. He'd seen it work here; had seen it work exactly the same way in other places before he came here. The law was a tool of those who were already powerful. In this country it had fitted the hand of Tomahawk for many years. Now it would do as much for the 3Y.

Shorty could see the body now, crumpled where it had fallen. The dead man's horse had spooked away a hundred feet and stood eyeing the approaching riders warily, his ears pricked forward.

The body looked large for Kirk. Doubt momentarily stirred in Shorty. He tried to fight it down. Suppose he had made a mistake? Suppose this wasn't Kirk?

He drew rein not a yard from the body and looked down in the rapidly fading light. Suddenly the pit of his stomach was a knot of fear. The dead man wasn't Kirk; it was Matt Van Horn.

Shorty dismounted and whirled to face the others, partially hiding the body with his own. As he turned, he glimpsed Delfino Chavez standing silently in a clump of service-berry brush not fifty yards away.

In spite of the poor light, the wolfer was recognizable to Shorty by his ragged sheepskin coat and his battered black hat. Delfino, although almost entirely concealed by brush, apparently realized he had been seen. Probably he had depended too much on the thin dusk light. He ducked just as Shorty drew and fired. He could not tell whether he had

116

scored a hit or not, so he emptied his gun at the spot where he had seen the wolfer.

Then, snatching his rifle from the saddle boot, he ran with panicked speed toward the place where Delfino had ducked out of sight. He crashed into the service-berry clump and fell headlong. He scrambled to his feet and clawed through the entangling brush. It raked his face and scratched his hands, but he was like a wild man.

The rifle discharged accidentally as he fell a second time. He realized he was sobbing for breath, trembling as though in the grip of some unexplainable chill. He fought to his feet and automatically levered another shell into the chamber of the rifle.

The third time he fell, he sprawled over something soft and yielding. The pungency of crushed sage was in his nostrils. It was so dark now he could scarcely see, but here at his feet was a prone, twisted shape.

Sitting up, Shorty emptied his rifle into the inert body of Delfino Chavez. He was almost hysterical, but some deeply recessed part of his mind recognized the necessity for overcoming it. His panic would only intensify the panic that already infected the others. If he was to be a leader, he must not permit his followers to see fear, or even hesitation, in him.

He fought a brief battle with himself. Then he forced himself to his knees and rolled Delfino over on his back. He struck a match.

Shorty Hough had fought many a brawl with fists and impromptu weapons. He had beaten men until they were only shells of what they had been and he had left them, knowing they would never be the same again. That fact had never bothered him, but until tonight he had never killed, and now the sight of Delfino Chavez almost unnerved him.

One of Shorty's bullets had entered Delfino's head exactly between the eyes. Most of the others had apparently hit, too, for the front of Delfino's shirt, exposed by his open sheepskin, was sodden with blood.

The rifle bullets pumped into Delfino from close range had been unnecessary. The wolfer had been dead when he hit the ground.

The others had come up now, their horses circling the

117

clump of brush through which Shorty had charged. As Shorty got to his feet, Eli asked in a voice that did not sound like his, "Who is it this time?"

"Delfino Chavez."

Eli breathed, "Oh, my God."

Shorty leaped and, grabbing Eli's sheepskin coat, tumbled him out of the saddle. He reached down and yanked him to his feet. His voice cut like acid when he said, "What was I supposed to do, let him get away? He'd've been back at Tomahawk in two hours and then where d'you think we'd be? That ain't Kirk back there. It's Matt. Kirk's still alive."

A shocked silence greeted his words. Shorty said, "By God, you better listen to me and listen good! All of you. Them two have got to go over the rim. If they don't, they'll be found tomorrow, and the whole Tomahawk crew will be down on us. Henessy, too, maybe."

Eli sidled away until he was behind his horse. Then he said in a shaky voice, "Not me. I won't touch either one of 'em. I'm gettin' out of here."

Chet Tappan echoed his words. Even Luke Bartram, who usually supported Shorty volubly, began to edge away.

"All right, all right," Shorty shouted angrily, "leave 'em here! But you're fools. You're still thinkin' because I pulled the trigger I'm the one who'll pay. You're wrong as hell! You're all guilty! The tracks of your horses are around both bodies. You think Kirk can't read sign? You think he'll pick and choose when Tomahawk comes after us?"

Eli was broken. Shorty couldn't see his face, for it was full dark now, but he could tell by the old man's voice as he asked with pathetic uncertainty, "What are we goin' to do?"

Shorty knew he couldn't hold them here. They couldn't listen to anything he had to say with Delfino's sightless eyes staring up at them from the darkness. So he mounted and led out through the break in the fence. They followed silently. Shorty went on until he reached their cow camp. He dismounted and tied his horse, then went into the cabin and lighted the lantern.

The others followed, their faces set and pale. They sat down wearily and looked at Shorty as if hoping he had found some miraculous way out for them.

During the ride, Shorty had had time to think. All doubt

had left him. One Van Horn was out of the way, and Delfino could have been a dangerous man. No, he had no regrets for what had happened.

"Maybe you're over the shakes," he said, "and can listen to me. Right now there's only one man holdin' Tomahawk together. Kirk Van Horn. We got to get rid of him."

"What good'll that do?" Chet Tappan asked.

Shorty turned and snapped at him, "We get Kirk and we bust Tomahawk, that's what! We grab their range, and all of a sudden the law's on our side. I'm goin' to Jubilee to see Henessy. He'll listen. There's a dozen of us. We'll swear both of them killings was self-defense. We'll make it stick, all right. Luke, you take Eli's glasses and watch Tomahawk. You may have to wait a while, but sooner or later you'll get a chance to plug Kirk."

"Another killin'?" Eli said dismally.

"You got a better idea?" Shorty challenged. "You know a better way to cheat the rope? If you do, let's have it." Eli was silent, and Shorty went on, "We been talkin' about takin' Tomahawk range. Now, by God, it's ready for the takin' and we'll take it!"

Eli shook his head. He looked at the men sitting against the wall. They were his neighbors and he had been their leader for years. He wasn't now. They were looking to Shorty just as they had always looked to him, and he was as bad as the rest. He'd been manhandled by Shorty and he'd done nothing; he'd been given orders by Shorty and he'd obeyed them. What had brought this about?

He sat there studying Shorty Hough, the only man in the room who held no land and owned no cattle. Until Kirk's return, Shorty had been a mild and able man; then, suddenly, he had begun to change until now he had become a self-appointed leader, dangerous and fanatic.

Eli wanted to cry out, *Here's the man you ought to kill! Here's the one who'll wreck us all!* But he bit his lip, saying nothing. He saw the will to kill in Shorty's eyes. He wouldn't get halfway through his second sentence before he'd be dead.

He dropped his head into his folded arms, a bleak hopelessness ruling his mind. What Shorty said was true. It was too late to oppose him. They were in this now and could not back out.

Rachel Yockey, sitting up and waiting for her father's and Shorty's return, was oppressed by an almost overpowering foreboding. As time went on, the foreboding grew until it was close to panic.

She and Marge had prepared supper for the men shortly after dark. Now the meal was in the warming oven above the stove. Occasionally Rachel basted the venison roast to keep it from drying out, or stirred the mashed potatoes so a crust wouldn't form over them. The biscuits were already ruined, dry clear through and hard as rocks.

She moved restlessly around the kitchen, her mind returning to the question that had nearly driven her mad all evening. What had happened on Buck Point? Had the Salt Creek bunch shot it out with Kirk and the Tomahawk crew? Just at dusk she thought she'd heard gunfire up on top of the plateau, but the distance had been so great she hadn't been sure.

Suppose they had killed Kirk? With that thought, she began to daydream. She had realized ever since the meeting in the schoolhouse that she had lost Kirk, so that now she would have to use Shorty. She was sure she could handle him. He had believed her lie about Kirk just as everyone else had, but the difference was that he had used the lie to unite the Salt Creek men against Kirk, which was just what she had planned.

All right, she couldn't have Kirk. But she could still be mistress of Tomahawk, which was what she really wanted. She began counting her assets. There was the numerical strength of the Salt Creekers, which should be great enough to win the fight, with Guy Van Horn laid up. She was sure it would if Kirk were killed. Then, there was Shorty's brute-strength leadership, which he had demonstrated at the schoolhouse. It wasn't enough by itself but, guided by her brains, it would be. The thought pleased her. Kirk, she reflected bitterly, had never given her credit for brains. Well, she'd show him! She'd show them all. . . .

It was midnight before she heard her father and Shorty. Instantly she set to work setting the meal on the table. Outside she could hear them putting their horses away. It struck her as strange that they were so subdued, not talking and yelling at each other as they usually did.

120

When Eli came in, one look at his face started her heart to pounding. She asked, "Kirk?"

Eli shook his head. "Matt, and Delfino Chavez."

"Dead?"

He nodded.

"Who did it?"

"Shorty. But we're all in it."

Panic touched her. Kirk was the dangerous one, and he was still alive. "What are you going to do?"

He wouldn't look at her. Marge stood in the kitchen doorway, staring at her husband, horror in her eyes.

Rachel repeated sharply, "What are you going to do? Answer me!"

Eli didn't look up. Shorty came in, defiant and brazen; if he felt any sense of guilt for having murdered two men, he didn't show it. He said, "I'll answer your question. We're goin' to get Kirk. After that, takin' Tomahawk will be easy."

His eyes held hers, daring her to protest over the murder of a man she had planned to marry. She crossed the room to him and kissed him on the mouth. Not looking at her father, she said, "We've let the Van Horns run over us too long. It's time they were stopped. It's time we took back what belongs to us."

"They'll be stopped," Shorty said. "Stopped dead, by God!"

She felt the brute strength of his arms crushing her to him, and suddenly she found it attractive, his very brutality raising the old familiar desire in her. She raised her lips to his bruising kiss, her body molded against his, and she felt the animal hunger flooding through him.

It wouldn't be so bad, she told herself. A smart woman could direct even a brutal man like Shorty, as strong-willed as he was. And she would have Tomahawk. She would have all of Tomahawk to rule over. Like a queen. . . .

Eighteen

Kirk had expected Matt to ride back to Tomahawk before morning, and slept lightly, his door open, thinking he would hear his brother's steps on the stairs. When he woke at dawn, he realized immediately that he had not heard Matt come in.

He put on his shirt and pants, and stepped into the hall. He glanced into Matt's room. The bed had not been slept in.

He returned to his own room, trying to quiet the throbbing worry that had suddenly brought a fine film of sweat to his forehead. Damn it, he shouldn't have left Matt up there by the fence!

Still, maybe he had no reason to worry. Matt could have gone to the Cathedral Rim cow camp for a few hours' sleep. He might even have decided to stay at the fence all night in spite of Kirk's order not to remain that long.

Kirk tried to calm himself with the thought that Matt had gone stubborn and stayed out waiting to be relieved, but it wouldn't quite go down. Matt had showed unexpected courage last night when he'd insisted on staying; yet, a few hours along that fence was all anyone could expect of Matt, and it should have satisfied the demands he made upon himself.

Worry clung to Kirk's mind all through breakfast, though he tried not to let either Billy or Kate sense the fear that kept growing in him.

"Why ain't Matt up?" Kate asked.

"He didn't come in last night," Kirk said. "Probably figured it was easier to stay at the cow camp."

He finished quickly, avoiding Kate's questioning gaze. Leaving her dawdling over a cup of coffee, he crossed the yard to the corral. He kept reassuring himself by thinking that Matt wasn't one to go looking for trouble. Besides, he'd promised to come for help if anything happened.

But the fear that Matt had run into trouble grew steadily in Kirk. By the time he finished saddling his horse, he was trembling with apprehension. The truth was, that Matt was the last man on Tomahawk who should have been left to guard the fence.

As Kirk mounted, Billy ran toward him from the house, calling, "Where you going, Kirk?"

Kirk grinned at his younger brother. "Just going to take a look at the Buck Point fence."

Billy's eyes fastened on the Colt at Kirk's hip, then on the Winchester in the saddle boot. He cried out, "C'n I go with you? I can shoot!"

"Sure you can, but somebody's got to stay here and look after Pa and Kate."

He whirled his horse, leaving Billy standing there not sure whether he'd been complimented or just reminded that he was too young for the dangerous business at hand.

Kirk was halfway across the meadow when he saw Bianca break out of the timber, riding fast toward Tomahawk. He turned to intercept her. When he was close enough to see her expression, he felt the sudden weakness that the certainty of disaster brings to a man.

Before she quite reached him, she called, "Kirk, Dad didn't come back home last night!"

Both reined up, a dozen feet apart. She was very pale, her eyes looking as though she had not slept at all during the night. He said, "Delfino left us at your cabin. You mean he went out again?"

She nodded. "He was worried about Matt."

"No call to get worried. Chances are they both stayed at the cow camp."

"But he said he'd be back by ten or eleven and to keep his supper warm! When he didn't show up by then, I went to bed. I didn't think much about it. You know how he's always lived. He's never paid any attention to time. But this morning when I found he hadn't come in at all . . ."

Kirk nodded, masking the grim certainty that now gripped him. Matt and Delfino were both dead. He made no attempt to guess how or why. If only one had failed to come in, he would not have been so sure. But both of them . . .

He said, "I'll go have a look. You ride on to the house and keep Kate company."

She shook her head stubbornly. She said, her voice so determined that he didn't argue with her, "No, I'm going with you."

They took the same route he had traveled the day before with the crew, hurrying now, although Kirk was convinced that nothing would be changed by haste. Both Matt and Delfino were dead: The conviction rode with him, somber and inescapable.

The sun was well up by the time they reached the fence, dissipating the chill of early dawn. He heard the bawling of Salt Creek cattle, knowing that his K Bar cows and calves

123

were among them. He was relieved, for their bawling indicated they were still on the Buck Point side of the fence. Then he saw a small herd of twenty or thirty grazing in a small clearing, and he realized the fence had been cut, though probably only one short section of it.

They found Matt's body first, lying crumpled and broken just as it had fallen. Bianca cried out involuntarily, and Kirk said harshly, "Stay in your saddle." He stepped down and picked up Matt's hand. It was cold and stiff. Matt had been dead for hours.

When he straightened, he saw that Bianca had found her father's body. He ran toward her, wishing he could have saved her this.

When he reached the girl, she was kneeling in a clump of service-berry brush. Delfino lay on his back, a bullet hole between his eyes, his shirt brown and stiff with dried blood. He had been literally shot to pieces, but why? Any one of the half dozen bullets would have been enough.

Kirk stood looking down, torn between shock and a growing, outraged fury. Bianca began to tremble, to whimper almost soundlessly, like a child.

This was the work of a madman, of a man turned crazy by hate. And yet who could hate Delfino? He had been liked by everyone. Perhaps it had been fear instead of hate that had caused his death. He'd simply been in the wrong place at the wrong time and had seen too much.

With gentleness, Kirk pulled Bianca to her feet. Her face was white and blank with shock. He said softly, "Bee, he's gone. There's nothing you can do for him now."

Anger kept mounting in him, furious, deadly anger at the sheer brutality of this. He had no way of knowing how many men had been responsible, but from the tracks, he judged the entire Salt Creek bunch had milled around Delfino's body. It was hard to believe that some of them, Lew Warren and Chet Tappan and a few of the others, were capable of a murder as savage and brutal as this. But what about Shorty Hough? Luke Bartram? Eli Yockey? Yes, any one of these, or all three, could be guilty.

His arms were around Bianca's trembling body. Her head was against his chest. Shock still held her in its grip. She drew

124

her head back and looked at him. The expression in her eyes was like a cold hand suddenly gripping his heart.

He said, "We've got to take them home."

She nodded numbly. She wasn't crying. This was still shock, the awful impact of grim reality. Tears and a letting go would come later. She had been very close to Delfino. After this, life could never be the same for her. She would be desperately lonely. She couldn't live alone, but he wasn't sure she'd be willing to come to Tomahawk.

She was staring at him, her rigid face betraying the strict discipline under which she held herself. Suddenly Kirk realized she had not cried out for revenge.

Tenderness for her almost overcame him, and in that instant he knew he loved her, knew that he had always loved her. How could he have been this blind? Rachel had the ability to fire desire in him, but he'd always been plagued by doubts about her. This feeling he had for Bianca was so much greater, for it included tenderness and a desire to give of himself that he had not known he was capable of feeling for any woman.

But he couldn't tell her now. He released her and lifted Delfino in his arms, startled at the old man's slight weight. He laid the body gently across Bianca's saddle. "We'll lead the horses to the cow camp. We can leave Matt and Delfino there and send a wagon back for them."

With equal care he loaded Matt upon his own horse. Walking, exertion, would be good for Bianca.

At the cow camp, he carried both bodies into the cabin and laid them on bunks. Shutting the door, he went outside and helped Bianca into her saddle.

They rode back together, the warm May sun beating down upon them, slowly driving the chill of shock from their bodies. A burden of guilt lay heavily on Kirk because he had let Matt stay, but it gradually faded. Matt wouldn't want him to blame himself.

Matt had made his decision to stay with full knowledge of what might happen, yet he had still been man enough to take the risk. He would not have wanted Kirk to ride herd on him, for that was what Guy had done for all of Matt's life and it was what Matt was fighting to escape. He wouldn't have wanted Delfino to come back, either.

125

If blame lay anywhere, it lay with Guy Van Horn, who had never allowed Matt to prove himself as he had felt obliged to do last night. But fixing blame could serve no purpose now. Besides, the only man who could really be blamed was the one who had pulled the trigger.

They reached Tomahawk's hay meadows before Bianca said, "What are you going to do?"

"I'll send Billy for the preacher. I'll take a wagon back for Matt and Delfino myself. I suppose Delfino would want to be buried on Tomahawk, wouldn't he?"

"It's where he lived. I'm sure he would." She was silent for a moment, then she said, "What I meant was, what are you going to do about the man who killed them?"

"What do you want me to do?"

She frowned. "It's easier to say what I don't want you to do. If you were Guy, you'd take the crew and go down to Salt Creek and clean house—kill every one of them you could find, and burn their houses. I don't want you to do that."

"What, then?"

She bit her lip. "Dad always said this kind of trouble would come eventually. He said it was because we didn't have any law, except Guy Van Horn's law, and now we don't have that." She looked at him in desperation. "Somebody's got to bring law to this country. Maybe you can—the kind of law we ought to have, the kind that means something to everybody."

He stared at her, thinking that Delfino Chavez, an ignorant wolfer who could barely read the newspaper, had given Bianca a standard by which she could live and which would give her courage to face whatever came to her. Delfino Chavez had had a great store of wisdom and faith, but Guy Van Horn, for all of his wealth and power, had never possessed either.

Kirk had no great trust in the sheriff, but Henessy was all the law there was. He said, "All right. As soon as the funeral's over, I'll go see the sheriff. The Salt Creek bunch will expect us to move today. A little sweating will be good for them."

After that he rode with her in silence to the door of the great house. He helped her down gently and went with her

126

inside where he turned her over to Kate. And still she had not wept.

On the day following the funerals, Kirk left Tomahawk at sunup, telling the two men who had been feeding bulls in the meadow to stay close to the house. He wasn't ruling out an attack by the Salt Creekers, although it was not probable.

He took the horseback trail to Jubilee, the same trail he had traveled with Matt the day of his mother's death. It seemed a long time ago. A lot had happened since then.

Guy's stroke had changed the world for the Van Horns, and Kirk kept thinking that if it hadn't been for the stroke, Matt might not have died. Guy would not have allowed him to stay at the fence.

Yet the more Kirk pondered it, the more he became convinced that Matt's choice had been a wise one. Matt had been bitterly dissatisfied with himself, so he had done what he had to do, the only thing he could have done.

Kirk reached Jubilee and tied in front of the sheriff's office, but Henessy wasn't there. "You'll find him at O'Mara's," the jailer told him. "He's been talkin' about goin' out to your place, but he ain't gone yet."

"Then he's heard about Delfino and Matt?"

"Who ain't?"

Angered, Kirk swung around and left the building. Everybody had heard, he thought, and everybody was waiting to see what he would do. Apparently no one even expected Henessy to do anything. Bianca had been right. The law on the plateau had been Guy Van Horn's so long that Henessy didn't even consider interfering. Or was it something else?

Henessy was bellied up against the bar in O'Mara's, his fingers toying with a shot glass. He nodded briefly at Kirk.

O'Mara asked, "What's yours, Kirk?"

Kirk said, "Nothing. I'm here to see Red." He studied the sheriff, sensing that the man was uncomfortable. "We've had a couple of murders, Red. Isn't the sheriff's office interested?"

"Heard about that," Henessy admitted, raising the glass to his mouth. His Adam's apple bobbed once as he gulped the drink. He put the glass down and wiped his mouth with the back of his hand. "I'm sorry about it, Kirk, mighty sorry."

"Being sorry ain't enough. What are you going to do?"

"Do?" Henessy squinted at him. "Why, boy, you've got to understand that these things take time." He turned away from Kirk. "O'Mara, your whiskey gets worse every damned year. Break out that bottle you keep for the Van Horns. Gimme a drink out of it."

Kirk felt blood rushing to his head, and rashness with it. He wouldn't have come here at all if it hadn't been for Bianca. This wasn't Guy's way. Maybe it shouldn't be his.

"What the hell's eating you, Red?" O'Mara said plaintively. "You never complained before."

Something was wrong here, Kirk realized. He knew that if Guy had been running Tomahawk, Henessy wouldn't even have been in town. He'd have been out fishing and he'd have stayed out until the trouble was over. The very fact that he was here revealed his position. He wasn't Tomahawk's man any more. He was even hostile to Tomahawk, as his words to O'Mara made unmistakably plain. Henessy probably was figuring that Tomahawk was dead.

And if Henessy was figuring that way, someone must have been talking to him—probably Shorty Hough.

Kirk grabbed the sheriff by the shoulder and yanked him around. Henessy swore, his hand dropping to the grips of his guns. "Keep your hands off me," he said thinly.

"Then don't turn your damned back on me!" Kirk glared at him. "Time's something I haven't got. And you've used up yours. You've been sitting on your butt now for two days doing nothing, and that's plain enough for me. But I want you to say it, Red. I want O'Mara to hear it, too."

Henessy growled, "There's lots of troubles in the country besides Tomahawk's. I'll get to yours when I ain't so busy."

Kirk wheeled to O'Mara. "Plain enough, isn't it? He's too busy to look into a couple of murders." He turned back to Henessy, speaking softly now. "I'm not too busy, Red." He swung away and tramped to the door. There he turned and said, "Know something, Red? You just lost the next election. Shorty Hough won't be around to cast his vote."

He went out of the saloon, relieved as well as angered, for now he could proceed directly as he wished.

The law might come to mean something in this country someday, but it wouldn't as long as Red Henessy wore the star. That was sure.

128

Kirk took the road downcountry from Jubilee, then swung up out of the valley onto the trail across the low, cedar-covered hills toward Tomahawk. It was warm, giving promise of blistering days to come. Sun-heat rose in shimmering waves from the dry, rounded hills. The sky was cloudless, blue as a robin's egg.

By ordinary standards, it was a fine day, a welcome change after the cold winds of spring. Kirk was hardly in the mood to enjoy it. The more he thought about Red Henessy, the more his anger grew. The sheriff considered Tomahawk dead with Guy laid up, and that made him as wrong as a man could be.

He rode for about fifteen minutes over the fragrant cedar hills, occasionally crossing a flat of sagebrush nearly as high as his head. He saw a few fresh cattle tracks, and swung to follow them.

Later, at a drying spring, he picked up two Tomahawk cows with calves, and a yearling steer. Driving them ahead of him, he angled back to the trail.

The calves scampered back and forth, waving their spotlessly white, ridiculous tails like banners. Presently they tired of this and settled down to plodding steadily behind their mothers. Somehow this little bunch had escaped spring roundup. Kirk took them in because they wouldn't thrive on this low winter range the way they would on the higher plateau. Besides, the calves were slick-eared and had to be branded.

He rode moodily, thinking of Matt and Delfino. His fury over their wanton murder had lost its wildness. Now it was like a steadily glowing bed of coals that nothing could extinguish. Nothing, that was, but the death of the murderer.

Damn Henessy anyway! Damn a man who straddled a fence and jumped the way his self-interest lay. Well, if Henessy couldn't find the killer—and he wouldn't if he didn't try—then, by heaven, Tomahawk could!

Ahead of Kirk lay a long ridge, the top of which was a jumble of dun sandstone outcroppings. The trail angled up the ridge, well worn by the countless Tomahawk riders who had used it to go to town and return.

The cattle took it willingly enough, lining out here in single file. One of the calves lagged, and Kirk swung his rope end, lightly tipping the calf's rump with it. The animal bawled and spurted ahead, afterward traveling with his head against his mother's flank.

Kirk was reasonably sure that Shorty Hough had been the man who had dropped Delfino and Matt up there by Cathedral Rim. He wondered if Shorty would run, or stay and follow through with his grab for Tomahawk range. He decided there was no question about his staying, or Henessy wouldn't have reacted the way he had.

Kirk was vastly disillusioned, too. The tracks near the fence had indicated that all or most of the Salt Creek bunch had been present at the time of the killings, or immediately afterward. And Kirk had thought he had some friends among them. Eli Yockey and Chet Tappan, at least, and he had been reasonably sure of Lew Warren. Now he realized he had no friends on Salt Creek. Bianca had been right in saying he did not belong with them.

Still, he couldn't believe they had all acquiesced in the murders. That left him only one alternative. There simply hadn't been enough moral courage in a single one of them to try and prevent the killings or deal out justice to the killer afterward.

He was two-thirds of the way to the top of the bluff now. The wind was blowing toward him out of the north directly off the top. Suddenly his horse's ears pricked and the animal raised his head and drew breath into his lungs as a preliminary to a shrill whinny.

Shock traveled through Kirk, coupled with the instant realization that he had been careless, perhaps fatally so. Someone was up there in that jumbled pile of rocks, and Kirk had a good guess why he was there.

Without hesitation, he flung himself out of his saddle, seizing the rifle stock that protruded from the boot. The rifle caught, but his savage yank tore the scabbard loose and the rifle slid out.

The horse spooked away, sliding on his haunches down the steep, gravelly slope. The cattle lunged ahead, startled, just as the flat, wicked bark of a rifle sounded up there among the rocks. The bullet whanged away off a boulder, singing until its sound was lost in distance. Kirk saw a small puff of smoke that quickly drifted away on the wind.

There was no cover here, nothing but bare ground and scrub brush less than a foot high. Kirk felt naked and exposed. He slid his rifle out before him, sighting loosely on the spot from which the puff of smoke had come.

It came again, and Kirk fired instantly. He was rewarded by a tiny geyser of dust flying off the rocks at which he had aimed.

One of the cows ahead of him bawled with fright. Her hindquarters went down, and she frantically tried to drag herself ahead with her forelegs. She failed, lost her footing, and rolled down the slope, bellowing.

The man must be scared and nervous, to have missed so widely. The range was less than two hundred yards.

The unseen shooter could not afford to wait much longer. Tomahawk lay just over this ridge not more than half a mile away. Someone there might hear the shots. If they were heard, one of the Tomahawk men would be on his way now to investigate. The ambusher up in the rocks would know; he would know, too, that he had to get this over and be gone.

Kirk felt like a clay duck in a shooting gallery. The rifle barked again, its sound echoing back from the hills toward town. This time the bullet lifted a shower of dirt and flung it into Kirk's face.

Suddenly, a towering rage came over him. He lay still, cowering against the ground for a moment, letting the fury have its way, letting it rise like a forest fire crowning the trees. It grew and mounted until it became a reckless, unthinking force. It brought Kirk surging to his feet and sent him in a plunging charge up the steep slope directly toward the ambusher's place of concealment.

The bushwhacker lost his head. The rifle banged away as swiftly as the man could work the lever. Bullets tore into the ground at Kirk's feet. They whistled over his head. They ricocheted off the rocks nearby and sang viciously until they passed out of hearing range.

131

But Kirk didn't slow and he didn't stop. All sense of caution was gone. He could think of nothing except that there in front of him was the man who had murdered Matt and Delfino. Or, at least, this man would know who had. Kirk wanted the man's throat in his hands. He wanted it more than he had ever wanted anything in his life before.

He stumbled and fell, jumped up and charged on up the slope. His lungs labored and his head felt light. His body was hot and sweat poured down his dusty face.

He didn't even realize it when the man stopped shooting. He had no ability to reason, no rational process to tell him. All he knew was hate and this blinding rage.

He reached the top of the ridge. His lungs were afire; his breath came in choking gasps. He lunged toward the spot where the bushwhacker had been, fell, and rose and stumbled forward.

He would have killed with his bare hands if the man had been there. But the ambusher was gone. Kirk could see beyond the ridge, could see him on his horse climbing the next one. He was leaning forward low over his horse's withers. He had a quirt in his hand and was belaboring the animal's rump with it. His spurs raked the horse's sides.

Kirk squinted, trying to clear his blurred vision. *Who was it?*

He had to stop him, turn him! He fell to one knee and brought up his rifle. Drawing a careful bead, he tried to steady his arms that were shaking from the exertion of a few minutes before. He squeezed the trigger.

His bullet struck a clump of sagebrush immediately in front of the fleeing rider. Perhaps it broke a branch and drove a splinter into the horse's chest. He couldn't be sure what happened, but the animal set his feet and skidded to a halt. He reared, almost unseating the rider, then turned and clawed frantically straight up the ridge.

But in the instant he reared, in that briefest of instants while he was motionless, Kirk got a good look at the man's face as he turned to stare back. It was Luke Bartram.

Suddenly the strength went out of Kirk's arms. He nearly dropped the rifle. His heart was thudding painfully inside his chest.

The urgency of the moment was gone. He knew who had

ambushed him and tried to kill him, but he couldn't go back down the slope, get his horse and ride in pursuit with any hope of success. Besides, there was no need for it. Bartram would pay when the time came.

Kirk watched Bartram ride along the top of the ridge until he was a mile above the buildings at Tomahawk. Then the rider crested the ridge and stopped while he scanned the valley below him. After that he rode out of sight to cross the valley and head again for Buck Point.

There was no hurry. Let Bartram worry about what had happened. There were a lot of fearful men down on Salt Creek, Kirk was sure. Let Bartram add himself to their number. Let them live in mortal terror of Tomahawk's reprisal.

Grimly Kirk made his way back down the slope to his horse. He mounted, and rode to where the crippled cow lay. He shot her between the eyes, then roped her calf, which was trying to nuzzle her udder, and dragged the animal up the hill.

He picked up the other cow and calf, and the steer, halfway to the top of the ridge. The calf at the end of the rope joined them and ran ahead of Kirk's horse.

This was the way Kirk came into the yard at Tomahawk. He dismounted and led the orphan calf to the barn. Old Jake, the choreman, could put it on one of the milk cows. After that Kirk shoved the cow and the other calf and the steer through a gate. Beyond, the way to the plateau top lay open. Then he made his way wearily to the house.

Twenty

Guy was sitting on the porch in Kate's rocking chair as Kirk approached. There was something tenacious about his mute eyes. Kirk stopped and looked down at him, still seething with anger. Guy had probably heard the shots, had guessed their meaning, and had been unable to call out for someone to investigate. Perhaps he had even seen Luke Bartram's figure skylined at the top of the ridge. Kirk felt a moment's

133

pity for his father, realizing what it must be like to want to do something so desperately and be unable to do it.

"Luke Bartram ambushed me on the other side of the ridge," Kirk said. "Hit one of the cows I was bringing in. Then he ran."

Guy's face twisted helplessly with a futile effort to speak but no words came. Suddenly he blinked his eyes, tears of frustration running down his cheeks.

"You think nothing's being done," Kirk said. "Or that nothing's going to be done. Well, you're wrong. Whoever killed Matt and Delfino is going to pay. Luke Bartram's going to pay. I did what I had to do today. I laid it in Red Henessy's lap and he won't lift a hand. All right, Tomahawk's been killing its own snakes for a long time. No reason we can't keep on doing it, is there?"

Doubt still showed in Guy's eyes, but it was fading. Kirk went on into the house. Kate had insisted that Bianca come to Tomahawk after Delfino's death, and now the two women were in the kitchen. Kirk looked at Bianca and saw that she had been crying. She looked drained and weak. He felt a surge of compassion for her, and crossed the room to her. She came into his arms and began to weep again. He patted her shoulder awkwardly.

She drew away, fighting her tears. "What did the sheriff say, Kirk?"

"He beat around the bush," Kirk said bleakly. "Turned his back on me. He won't do anything because he thinks Tomahawk's through. It's my guess Shorty Hough's been to see him and Henessy's going to play it careful till he finds out whether the Salt Creekers are going to be the power Shorty aims they will."

Her shoulders slumped. Kirk said, "Delfino was your father, but he was my friend, and Matt was my brother. Whoever killed them won't get away. I promise you that, Bee."

His face was hard set. She glanced up at him, but she made no protest. She turned and began helping Kate prepare supper.

Kirk watched her with awakening perception. There was tremendous strength of will and character in Bianca, but there was acceptance, too. She'd never try to mold a man,

134

to bend him to fit her wishes and desires. No, Bianca would understand him and the things he had to do.

Kate brought him a cup of coffee. He kept on watching Bianca, excitement stirring in him. He wondered why he hadn't felt this before. He loved her and he wanted to tell her, but this was hardly the time. He sipped his coffee thoughtfully. Outside the sun sank behind the plateau to the west. The sky turned gray.

Kirk helped Kate carry Guy in from the front porch. They brought him into the kitchen and set him down at the table. Guy glared at Kate and then at Kirk. As Kirk went outside to wash, he remembered how Guy had always relieved his temper by explosive words and acts, but now his eyes were his only means of showing his feelings.

Frank Surrency rode in, put his horse away, and joined Kirk at the pump. He said, "There's Salt Creek cattle strung all over the damned plateau—as far east as Horse Ridge, and as far south as Twin Springs."

Kirk nodded. Surrency studied him carefully, then asked, "What you going to do?"

"Tomorrow we'll gather up the crew. We'll have a round-up, just like fall roundup. We'll push everything that belongs on Salt Creek back on Buck Point and fix the fence."

Surrency's face brightened. "You figure on trouble?"

Kirk smiled thinly. "You bet I do."

Surrency dried his face and ran a comb through his hair. He followed Kirk toward the house, asking, "What're we supposed to do?"

"You're on Tomahawk range doing what you're told to do," Kirk said. "If anyone interferes, defend yourself."

Surrency's face creased into a grin. "That's what I wanted to hear."

They went into the kitchen and sat down at the table. Kate stopped in the midst of her preparations to say with dismay, "Lordy, I clean forgot the eggs."

Snatching up a shawl, she lighted a lantern and hurried outside with it in one hand and the egg bucket in the other. Bianca smiled at Kirk.

"She's proud of the way the hens are laying. She's doubled their production since she's been here. She'd no more leave the eggs overnight than she'd forget to feed the chickens."

135

Outside the wind had started up again. Kirk could hear sand pelting against the window, could hear the wind sighing in the eaves of the house.

It was full dark now, and silent in the kitchen as they waited for Kate to return. The lamp flickered as a breeze from a partly open window struck it. Bianca rose and closed the window.

A vague uneasiness touched Kirk. He wished that Tomahawk's whole crew wasn't out on the range. If Luke Bartram had been bold enough to ambush him practically in Tomahawk's back yard, it was possible that the whole Salt Creek bunch might strike at Tomahawk itself. He scowled, knowing he had assumed too much. He had gone on the belief that they wouldn't have the temerity to attack. Now, suddenly, he wasn't so sure.

He started to get up from his chair when a chill ran down his spine. From outside he heard Kate's scream, shocking because he had never heard her scream and had never expected her to. She just wasn't a screaming woman. He was halfway to the door before it died away. His gun was in his hand, and as he burst outside, his thumb eased back the hammer to full cock.

Frank Surrency was close behind him. Kirk called back over his shoulder, "Bee, shut that door and stay inside."

The door closed. Bianca knew how to do what was needed without argument and without delay. He was willing to bet that the first thing she'd do after she left the door would be to find a gun and load it.

He sprinted across the yard, thankful there was no moon. He could hear Kate yelling. It sounded as though a hell of a battle was being fought inside the chicken house. Chickens squawked and screeched, bodies hit the wall with enough force to shake the frame building. And over all of it was Kate's enraged voice.

Kirk slid to a halt beside the barn, thirty feet or so from the hen house. It was possible the Salt Creekers were all around the place. Kate might have surprised one of them in the chicken house. He might have sneaked in there to fire it as a diversion before the attack.

"See anything, Frank?" Kirk asked as Surrency pulled up beside him.

"Not a damned thing." Surrency's breath came fast. "All I know is we got to get Kate out of there."

"Wait a minute." Kirk caught his arm. "Kate's doing all right."

His eyes had become accustomed to the darkness now, and by the faint starlight, he could see the shadowy bulk of the hen house. If there were men out there, they were standing close to the building. His glance swung again, looking for horses, but he saw nothing. On the other side of the barn the horses were going wild in the corral, stampeding around it at a dead run.

The horses were a tip-off for Kirk. He relaxed and began to chuckle. Surrency jerked free from Kirk's grasp. "This ain't no damn joke! We've got to get her out of there: you take the right side and I'll take the left."

He ran across the yard, Kirk following. As he ran, the hen house door burst open and chickens poured out; they squawked and flapped, scattering feathers in their wake.

It was dark inside the building, for the lantern had gone out. Kate continued to screech curses, and Kirk heard her egg bucket banging against something that grunted heavily every time the bucket struck.

A dark shape catapulted through the door. Kirk shouted, "Don't shoot, Frank. It could be Kate."

"That sure as hell ain't Kate!" Surrency shouted.

"Don't shoot!" Kirk called sharply.

Apparently Surrency didn't hear. Flame speared from the muzzle of his gun. The dark shape veered heavily but swiftly, and came directly toward Kirk.

Another figure rushed through the door, this one unmistakably Kate Gorman. She screeched, "Dammit, I'll learn you to come snooping around my hen house. I'll learn you, you thieving varmint."

Eli the bear shambled past Kirk, traveling with the speed of an express train. He tripped on a Fresno lying beside the barn and rolled like a ball for fifteen feet. Then he got up and disappeared into the darkness.

Suddenly Kirk bent double, laughing. He wanted to call to Surrency that it was just Eli. But he couldn't get his breath long enough to say a word.

Kate stood there cursing the bear. Finally Kirk straightened up and leaned against the wall, finding strength to say, "Put your gun up, Frank. It was only Eli."

Kirk crossed to the hen house and found the lantern, still chuckling. He lighted it and viewed the havoc inside the building. Eggs were broken all over the floor and in the nests. He went outside, holding the lantern up to look at Kate. There was egg smeared on her dress. He tried to compose his face, but laughter broke out of him again.

"What'd he do, Kate, throw 'em at you?"

Kate's face was livid. "Damn it, Kirk, maybe you think this is funny, but . . ."

She choked, looking at him helplessly. Then the fury left her, and the corners of her wide mouth began to twitch. She started to laugh as hard as Kirk.

Grinning, Frank Surrency said, "You know, that bear did look like old man Yockey. I thought the whole damn bunch from Salt Creek was here."

Kirk chuckled. "So did Kate, Frank, so did Kate." But as he turned toward the house, the thought struck him that the attack they'd thought was being made might still happen. He'd stand guard just to be safe.

Twenty-One

Kirk went to bed at the same time Kate and the others did, but as soon as the house was quiet, he rose and went downstairs, carrying his boots so he wouldn't disturb anyone. Shrugging into his sheepskin coat, he went outside. As he passed the bunkhouse, he smelled the aroma of a pipe, and called softly, "Frank?"

"Uh huh. I figured it wouldn't be a bad idea to keep watch. Saw the sun glint on something up at the top of the ridge west of here late this afternoon."

"Then they're watching us."

"Wouldn't be surprised."

Kirk sat down on the step beside him, thinking that they might have been watched ever since Matt's and Delfino's bodies had been found. Certainly Bartram knew he had gone to Jubilee today.

"You go on to bed, Frank. I'll watch."

Surrency hesitated. "Wake me up at midnight so I can take a turn?"

"All right."

Surrency got up and went into the bunkhouse. Ten minutes later he was snoring.

Kirk considered this evidence of Surrency's loyalty. In a sense Guy had not earned it, and yet in another sense he had. He had always been scrupulously fair with his men. And, Kirk supposed, they admired the very harshness in Guy that made him so difficult to live with. Certainly they respected him. Guy was, Kirk knew, an outstanding specimen of a vanishing breed of men, conquerors of wilderness who were brutal and implacable because they had to be.

Out in the hills a wolf pack howled, reminding Kirk of Delfino. For a while he was depressed, missing the old wolfer, and knowing how miserable Bianca must be. Then his anger began to rise.

Guy's way would have been to gather the crew and storm down into Salt Creek Valley the moment the murders were discovered. Kirk knew Guy was disappointed because that hadn't been done. And yet Kirk believed one man had done the killing and he would continue to believe it until he had proof he was wrong. It was not his nature to exact payment from a whole group for an act committed by a single one of their number.

He was aware, too, that times were changing, a fact that Guy would never have admitted. The days of high-handed justice dealt out by cattle barons were passing. Kirk had felt a need to give the law its chance. Red Henessy had passed on it, but Kirk felt better for having given it to him.

The night hours passed, but Kirk was not sleepy, so he waited until almost two before calling Frank. Afterward he went into the house and dozed until dawn.

Immediately after breakfast Surrency rode west and Bianca south to find and pull in the Tomahawk crew. Surrency was gone all day, but Bianca returned about noon. Kirk stayed at Tomahawk, afraid to leave the ranch guarded only by Billy and the old choreman.

Several times during the morning he caught the reflection of sunlight on something bright atop the ridge to the west. It was the same thing Frank Surrency had seen, and could be nothing but the sun on binocular lenses.

Kirk marked the place carefully in his mind. He thought grimly, *Stay there, my friend. Tomorrow you and I will have a talk.*

All day the crew drifted in, by ones and twos and occasionally in larger groups. In late afternoon it occurred to Kirk that this sudden activity at Tomahawk undoubtedly was something the hidden watcher would report. The man might be gone by morning.

So Kirk saddled a horse and rode out quietly, saying nothing to anyone and keeping to the concealment of the buildings as long as he could. He angled away from the direction he intended to take and presently reached the timber.

He knew every inch of Tomahawk's vast range, but he knew the area immediately surrounding its meadows and buildings best of all. As a boy he had lain many times in the very spot where the watcher now lay, not missing any of the activity in the ranch yard below. And he knew exactly how to approach it without being seen.

He traveled in heavy timber for nearly fifteen minutes, took a steady climb, then dropped into a deep ravine. Presently he began to circle until he was half a mile behind the watcher's position. There he left his horse and continued on foot.

Savageness had been building steadily in him, and he realized suddenly how much effort waiting and reporting the murders to Henessy had taken. He smiled grimly, thinking there was more of Guy in him than he had realized. His own inclination had been to do exactly what Guy would have done, and it had been hard to hold back.

Now a sense of deep satisfaction came to him. The waiting was almost done. He thought of Matt, who, in staying to guard the fence, had so nearly achieved independence from Guy and gained his long-delayed self-respect. He thought of Delfino, whip-lean and brown, who had been more of a father to him than Guy had ever been.

He moved like an Indian through the timber and brush, silent and sure. Angling back and forth, he cut the watcher's

140

trail and saw that it had been traveled several times the last two days.

Now, knowing he was not far from the watcher, he slowed and became more cautious. The sun was low in the west, low against the terrain behind him that lifted until it reached the drop-off at Cathedral Rim. Doubt began to plague Kirk. Suppose the watcher had left?

He relaxed with relief as he caught the smell of cigarette smoke carried along on the air. He moved very carefully then, and a moment later he could see the back of the watcher's head.

The man held a cigarette between his fingers. He was studying Tomahawk through his binoculars. It was Luke Bartram. The instant Kirk recognized the man, yesterday's fury seized him again and he abandoned all caution.

Brush crackled as he crashed through it. Bartram whirled, dropping the binoculars to the ground. The cigarette fell from his fingers as he grabbed frantically for the rifle leaning against a tree.

Kirk reached him with a rush. His foot went out in a looping kick and caught the rifle barrel just as Bartram's fingers closed on it. It flew away a dozen feet, struck a rock, and discharged.

Bartram straightened and backed away. Kirk, savagely furious, slapped him hard in the mouth. "You dry-gulching son of a bitch!"

Bartram, still not recovered from his surprise, said, "Hold on, Kirk. I . . ."

Kirk slapped him again, this time on the left ear, the sound of it sharp in the still air. The blow left a red mark on the side of Bartram's face. Anger sparkled in the man's pale eyes. "You can't—"

"Stop me, Luke! Stop me!" Kirk's hand went out again, connecting in the same place it had before.

Bartram came out of it, lunging at Kirk and sinking his fist hard into Kirk's belly. Kirk grunted, a savage pleasure coming into his eyes. Stepping back, he said, "Good, Luke! Fine!"

Bartram rushed him again. Kirk straightened him with a hard smash to his mouth. Bartram rolled his tongue over

141

battered lips and Kirk punched him again in the same place. This time Bartram spun back, tripped, and fell heavily.

Bartram raised on an elbow and looked up at Kirk. "Wait, now. I wasn't . . ."

"Shut up, Luke. You come to me or I'll come to you."

"You got a gun. If I start whippin' you, you'll use it."

"You whip me?" Kirk laughed, and unbuckling his gun belt, tossed it aside.

Bartram lunged for the gun, but Kirk beat him to it. His eyes were off Bartram for a moment, a moment in which Bartram abandoned trying to reach the gun and grabbed up a boulder. Rolling to his back, he flung it at Kirk.

The rock struck Kirk in the side. Pain shot from the area like the sharp stab of a dozen knives. Suddenly all restraint was gone from Kirk.

He dived at Bartram, clawing for the man as he rolled aside. Bartram reached his feet, his shirt tearing in Kirk's grasp. He ran for his horse, Kirk a short two yards behind. When Bartram was within ten feet of his horse, Kirk dived for his legs. Bartram went down, rolling under the horse.

Kirk saw the animal hump up, saw him kick with a hind foot and heard Bartram grunt as the shod hoof connected. Then the horse, rearing against the pull of the bridle, broke the reins and galloped out of sight into the timber.

Kirk struggled to get to the man, but Bartram, on his back, lashed out with a spurred boot. The kick caught Kirk in the forehead, knocking him away.

Bartram scrambled to his feet and ran again toward Kirk's holstered revolver. Kirk tripped him. He got up and waited between Bartram and the gun. He said between his teeth, "You're going to have to fight for it, Luke."

Bartram put his head down and tried to ram Kirk in the belly. Stepping aside, Kirk brought his right fist like a hammer against the back of Bartram's neck. The man went down and lay still.

Kirk went over and picked up his gun belt. He carried it to a tree and hung it up. Hearing a scramble behind him, he whirled to see Bartram on his feet.

Sanity was gone from Luke Bartram's face. His reddened eyes were wild with hatred; his lips were twisted and blood trickled from both corners of his mouth. He held a gnarled limb of a pine tree, club size, four inches thick at the heavy end.

He came toward Kirk in a heavy, flatfooted way. When he was within a step of Kirk, he swung the club. Kirk ducked and came in beneath the arc of the weapon. His right fist sank into Bartram's belly. Straightening, he saw that the club's momentum had brought Bartram half around, but his own second swing was already begun. His fist slammed into the side of the Salt Creek man's skull. The force of it drove Bartram to his knees.

There was animal rage in Kirk as he dived at Bartram. He landed astride his body. Bartram twisted as Kirk battered his face with wicked, short jabs. Bartram's face spread and turned bloody beneath Kirk's fists. He rolled his head from side to side, blood drooling from his mouth.

Bartram moaned helplessly as Kirk panted, "Who was it, Luke? Who killed them, Delfino and Matt?"

Bartram babbled, "He'll . . . he'll kill me!"

"Or I will now! What difference does it make?" Kirk continued to hammer the bloody face, leaning back to get a better swing.

Bartram choked, "Wait. I'll . . ." Kirk's fist stopped his words, smashing against his mouth.

Kirk drew his fist back again and held it. "Who was it?"

Bartram's eyes, nearly closed, were slits of pure panic. He licked his bruised lips. "It was Shorty, Kirk. Shorty done it."

Kirk drew a long breath. He had been sure that Shorty was the guilty one, but now he had the proof—all the proof he needed. He got up and stood, spraddle-legged and panting, dizzy and tired. He said, "Catch your horse and ride, Luke. Ride out of the country and don't see Shorty. Don't even stop at Salt Creek. Keep riding, or the next time I see you I'll treat you like I'd treat a stock-killing wolf."

Luke stared at him. He got to his feet, but could not come quite erect. There was malevolence in his bloodshot eyes. He said hoarsely, "You figure all you've got to do is to get Shorty. Well, you're wrong. The Buck Point fence is down. Tomahawk's a ranch without range and you don't have the men to take it back. You're licked."

Kirk didn't answer. Luke stared at him a moment more,

143

then turned and shambled in the direction his horse had gone, not looking back once.

Kirk picked up Luke's rifle. He took his own gun belt down from the tree where he had hung it and buckled it on; then he headed down the ridge to where he had left his horse.

Luke's statement had jolted him. He was no longer in the position of having merely to hold Tomahawk range. The Salt Creekers had moved in, they were in possession, and now Tomahawk had to regain it.

There was no doubt in him—and no hesitation. War had come to the high plateau. Tomorrow men would bleed and die in the high grass, in the richly green quakie pockets, in the brooding fragrant groves of spruce.

And he knew one thing more. Tomorrow Shorty Hough would die, or he himself would. One way or the other, tomorrow would see the end.

Twenty-Two

Kirk reached his horse in early dusk and mounted. He rode back to Tomahawk, taking a more direct, shorter route than he had followed coming here, and reached the house in the first, full dark of night.

He put his horse away and stopped at the pump to wash. Luke Bartram had not marked his face, but his knuckles were badly skinned, and he knew they would not escape Bianca's notice. Probably not Kate's, either.

The kitchen was full and boisterously noisy. In winter when the whole crew was in, they ate in the cook shack. But in summer when normally only a few men were around, they ate in the kitchen with the family. Tonight, since this was an unexpected break in their routine, they were being fed by Kate.

Kirk sensed a definite eagerness about all of them, and worry touched him. Again he wondered at their steadfast loyalty. Tomorrow night some of them might be dead. Did they realize this? Judging by their conversation, the possibility had not occurred to them. They didn't even mention tomorrow in their talk.

When they had eaten, they thanked Kate one by one, and led by Frank Surrency, filed out to the bunkhouse. Kirk called, "Early start in the morning," knowing that he'd have to warn them they were in for open warfare and dreading it.

Then Kirk was alone in the kitchen with Bianca and Kate and Guy. Billy, who even yet could not stand being near Guy, had already gone to bed.

Bianca, gathering up dishes from the long table, glanced at Kirk's knuckles and then at his face. She asked, "Who did you see when you rode out while ago?"

"Luke Bartram. He'd been watching the house with binoculars."

She waited, her eyes studying his face. He added, "I told him to get out of the country."

She murmured, "But not before you made him tell you what you wanted to know."

He glanced at her, thinking she had the right to know at least part of what Bartram had told him. He said, "Shorty Hough is the one."

She turned quickly from him, carried a load of dishes to the sink, and returned for another. From the way her gaze kept coming back to his face, he sensed that she knew his intentions, but he told himself that at least he could spare her the knowledge that he was up against long odds. He had no illusions about tomorrow. Outnumbered as Tomahawk was, it would be a close thing.

Kate clattered dishes around the sink angrily, but she didn't say a word. Kirk glanced at Guy and surprised his father studying him. The expression in Guy's eyes was unreadable, but Kirk thought it was compounded of bewilderment and anger.

Guy was wondering why he didn't get at it, why he didn't take the crew down into Salt Creek Valley and clean house. If Guy knew that the Salt Creek bunch was in possession up there at the Cathedral Rim cow camp, his expression might have been different, Kirk thought ruefully.

When the dishes were done and put away, Bianca took off her apron and went outside. After a moment Kirk followed. He wasn't afraid for tomorrow, and he felt no hesitation

145

about what he must do. Yet he recognized the possibility that he would not see Bianca again after tonight.

She had stopped at the edge of the porch and was looking up at the stars. Kirk stood beside her for a moment, then he said softly, "Bee, I love you. I should have known a long time ago, but I guess I was blind."

She turned to him and he took her in his arms with a poignant urgency. He held her close against his chest while her body shook with sudden sobs. When they finally stopped, he tipped her head up and kissed her warm, full mouth.

"Tomorrow will see the end of it, Bee," he said.

"And the end to you, too, maybe," she said bitterly. "I'm scared, Kirk. I'm terribly scared."

"There's no other way. Henessy's thrown in with Shorty. Or anyway he's keeping hands off till he sees which way the wind blows." He paused, then added, "Either we go to them or they'll come to us. It's gone too far to settle it by talk."

He took her in his arms again, a sudden wild idea taking shape in his mind. There might be a way. There might!

She responded with a fire that made his heart beat fast with excitement. It was startling and pleasing to Kirk.

He asked hoarsely, "Bee, why did I wait until now?"

"It doesn't matter," she whispered. "It doesn't matter now."

He forced himself to step away from her. He said, "Tomorrow."

"Yes, tomorrow," she breathed, and whirled and fled into the house, slamming the door behind her and leaving him to wonder at her precipitate action. Was she bitter? Or without hope? Or only desperately frightened? It must be the latter, for she loved him; he was sure of it.

Kirk made a cigarette with shaking fingers. Why the devil had he wasted so much time? When he finished rolling the cigarette, he flipped it, unlighted, into the dark yard. He turned, and going into the house, climbed heavily to his room. The idea he'd had was wild and dangerous. It probably had little chance to succeed, but it was all he had, and it would have to do.

Dawn was a thin, gray streak outlining the ridges to the east when Kirk came into the yard the following morning. The air was chill and clear, fragrant with the smell of sage and spruce and cedar. Frank Surrency came from the bunk-house, gravely regarding Kirk's face.

"Luke tipped their hand last night," Kirk said, "although we knew. They've got our range and they intend to hold it. Chances are they'll fort up in one of our cow camps and we'll have a hell of a job rooting them out." Surrency nodded, and Kirk went on, "The boys ought to know what they're getting into."

"They know," Surrency said. "They can add two and two."

"We're outnumbered."

"They know that, too," Surrency said, "but numbers ain't everything."

Kirk felt a glow of gratitude. "All right, Frank. Let's figure it out. What will they expect us to do?"

"Only one of two things we can do," Surrency answered. "We'll have to split up, gather the Salt Creek cattle and chouse 'em back onto Buck Point; or we'll hunt till we find the bastards. Chances are they've forted up in the Cathedral Rim cow camp cabin. If they have, they'll figure on us rushing 'em."

Kirk nodded. "That's the way I'd call it. But the point is they won't know which we're going to do, so they'll have to cover both angles. That means they'll send out one or two scouting parties. The main bunch, including Shorty, will stay at the cow camp till they hear what we're up to."

"That's the size of it," Surrency agreed.

"Then we'll stay bunched. We'll poke around until we find one of those scouting parties and we'll start on them. The only chance we've got is to polish 'em off before the others get to them."

Frank Surrency nodded approvingly, but he kept studying Kirk as though expecting more. When Kirk didn't add anything, he said, "There's something else on your mind. Let's have it."

Kirk looked away. "Nothing else."

Surrency plainly didn't believe him. He returned to the bunkhouse and a few moments later re-appeared with the crew, frowning thoughtfully. They trooped into the kitchen where Kate and Bianca had breakfast on the table. They ate silently and as silently filed out afterward. There was tension in all of them, but no hesitation and no reluctance.

147

The wrangler ran in the horses and the men began roping out their mounts. Kirk caught his own, saddled and waited silently by the corral gate for the men to get ready.

Surrency came to stand by his elbow. In a low voice, he said, "Kirk, I think I know what you're up to. If I'm right, you're a bigger damn fool than I thought you was. Let me go with you."

Kirk shook his head. Gray light lay over the yard now. Kirk said, "No. You stay with the crew. They'll need you. I won't need any help. When I show up at the cow camp, Shorty and whoever's with him will figure the whole outfit's with me."

"Like hell . . ."

"Stay with the crew," Kirk said again, and this time Surrency let it go, but his eyes showed that he was still worried.

Kirk rode away, the crew following. He didn't go near the house, but he did raise a hand to Bianca, Guy, Kate and Billy who had gathered on the front porch. Bianca must have made a signal to Surrency, for he turned and rode toward her. She came down the steps and met him twenty feet from the porch. They were talking as Kirk rode on into the gloom of early dawn. He supposed briefly that Bianca was asking Frank to look out for him, and he knew that Frank would soon catch up.

Bianca was crying when Surrency rode up to her. She brushed impatiently at her tears, and asked, "Frank, what's he going to do?"

"Nothin' foolish, if I can help it."

"Can't you stop this, Frank?"

"He's the boss, Miss Chavez." Surrency glanced at Guy, knowing his words would carry to where the older man sat. He added, "And a damn good one, too."

The light was better now and Surrency could see Guy's expression plainly. There was shame in his eyes. His mouth twisted in a desperate effort to speak. Failing, his eyes pleaded with Surrency.

Kate looked at Guy, her own eyes filling with tears that she did not bother to brush away. She said, "He's your son, Guy. He's got all your guts and none of your orneriness. You sired a man when you sired him."

Guy's eyes were grateful, as though thanking her for saying the words he could not say himself.

Surrency stood there a moment more, looking from one to the other. In Bianca's face he saw terror and dread, but he saw resolution, too, and he sensed what she intended to do.

He mounted, whirled, and crossed the yard to the corral at a plunging lope. Leaning down, he shot the bar on the corral gate and swung it wide. Riding in, he hazed the remaining horses out through the gate and watched as they thundered away.

He rode off without a backward glance, ignoring Bianca's cries as she ran after the loose horses. She'd meant to follow, but now she could not, at least not in time to interfere. Surrency put his mind to the trail ahead, knowing he had to catch Kirk and the others soon, and knowing, too, that there was no time to waste.

Twenty-Three

With Kirk at the head, Tomahawk rode in silence, climbing steadily from the valley floor toward the higher ground of the mesa's top. Kirk put out flankers on both sides to scout the ridge tops and watch for the Salt Creekers.

Surrency caught up just as the sun rose, tipping the higher points ahead with its rosy glow. He came up behind Kirk, but he did not speak.

An hour passed. Doubts began to grow in Kirk's worried mind. Had he guessed the strategy of the Salt Creek bunch correctly? What if he'd made a mistake? He thought of Bianca and Kate, of Guy and Billy back at the house. What if Shorty Hough and a band of Salt Creek riders circled and attacked the house?

He shook his head impatiently. He had gone over this carefully and had reached the only decision possible. Now he had to play it out.

His spirits jumped when he saw, outlined against the sky on his right, one of the flankers beckoning with an upstretched arm.

Kirk hipped around in his saddle and flung a pointing arm in the direction of the flanker. Almost like cavalrymen the Tomahawk riders wheeled and rode in a frontal line toward the signaling flanker. Their horses broke from a trot into a hard gallop.

Kirk's mouth was hard set with fierce determination. The Salt Creekers had attacked Tomahawk, had seized Tomahawk range and were holding it with guns. Today would decide whether they could hold it, or whether Tomahawk could take it back. He looked at the faces of his men, and in every one he saw the same dedication he felt. He saw no hint of wavering.

Their unquestioning loyalty told him something he realized he should have known all along—that his own loyalty had never really wavered in spite of his trouble with his father, in spite of his attempt to pull away from Tomahawk and build a ranch of his own. Tomahawk was more than a ranch; it was for him a way of life, one that was as much a part of him as his own right hand. It had taken trouble—and death— to teach him this, but he knew it now and he would never forget it again.

They thundered down through an aspen-choked ravine and up the far side, their horses leaping down-timber, scrambling up the steep slope with contagious enthusiasm.

The entire crew pulled to a halt as they reached the flanker. Kirk, with dust boiling up around his plunging horse, asked, "How many?"

"Eight or ten. I couldn't get an exact count because they were ridin' through timber."

Kirk turned to Surrency, triumph in his smile. He'd guessed right. But he had to be sure. He asked the flanker, "Shorty with 'em? Or Eli?"

"Neither one. I looked for them special."

The odds, then, were about even. Still, they weren't even at all when he remembered there was another band of Salt Creek men of approximately equal strength not far away. Certainly the other bunch would be within hearing distance of gunfire, which carried well on the high plateau. When they heard the sound of shooting, they'd come on the run.

Kirk rode close to Surrency. "I'm coming in with you. I think we can whip them fast if we surprise them. As soon as things are under control, I'm leaving. Don't waste time looking for me."

Worried, Surrency demanded, "What are you figuring on?"

"I'm going after Shorty."

Kirk kept the fury that was in him under strict control, but he was thinking now of Matt, and of Delfino, thinking how Shorty must have stood over Delfino and pumped bullet after bullet into the old wolfer's body. There was added reason in his decision to go after Shorty. He was the leader, the backbone of the entire Salt Creek bunch. With Shorty out of it, the fight would drain out of them like water out of a punctured canteen.

Surrency nodded doubtfully, then wheeled away. The crew rode behind him and Kirk, down through the quiet, sundappled timber. They crested another ridge, and saw below them the file of Salt Creek riders.

Kirk raised an arm. The crew halted behind him expectantly. He saw in their faces the loyalty men give their acknowledged leader. Guy Van Horn was helpless but Tomahawk still had a hand to guide it to its destiny.

A warm feeling spread through Kirk. Death might find him today. But if it came, he would die knowing that he'd found his place, that he'd filled his father's boots.

He flung an arm forward, and dug spurs into the sides of his horse. The animal leaped ahead, and behind him he heard the answering thunder of a dozen more. A yell broke out of his throat. This, too, was echoed from the throats of the Tomahawk riders.

Below, a shot racketed, followed by a volley that crackled like a string of firecrackers. A Tomahawk horse threw up his head, then crashed to the ground, rolling, momentarily pinning his rider beneath him. Looking back, Kirk saw the cowboy rise and hobble off in the dusty wake of the remaining horsemen.

Now Tomahawk guns were roaring all around Kirk. The men swept down into the draw in a yelling, pounding line. They piled through the demoralized Salt Creek men and rode on up the far slope where they halted and wheeled for a second charge.

Kirk saw three motionless bodies in the bottom of the draw. Tomahawk fire had been devastating. Then he realized that

151

the remaining Salt Creek men were down on the ground, firing steadily from the cover of rocks, down trees, dead horses—from the shallow ravine itself.

He yelled at Surrency, "They'll wipe you out if you charge again. Go down afoot, but keep under cover."

Surrency nodded. Sweat made little muddy rivulets down his dusty jaws. Kirk wheeled his horse and rode away. Behind him he could hear the sporadic firing as the fight continued.

He lay low over the neck of his horse, ignoring the branches that whipped and tore at his face, at his clothes. The horse responded, and the miles fell behind.

Yet now he began to doubt. He might have guessed wrong. Suppose Shorty wasn't at the cow camp, but with the second roving party of invaders? He gritted his teeth and spurred more savagely, thinking he couldn't be wrong. The winded, sweaty horse lunged frantically ahead. Now the land rose toward the high rim to the west, and the miles seemed to fall behind with exasperating slowness.

He pulled his revolver from its holster and reloaded carefully. Then, replacing it, he slipped it in and out several times to loosen it in the holster against the time when he would need it.

Once more he thought of Matt and Delfino, letting his anger run unchecked through his mind. He felt the blood pound in his head and he drove his flagging horse to greater speed.

Familiar with each foot of this trail, Kirk knew where he was every moment. As he approached the Cathedral Rim cow camp, his ears picked up the sounds of activity. His nerves tightened, but his tension was an inner thing which did not communicate itself to his body.

He had no illusions about the odds that faced him; there would be several men with Shorty. He knew that whatever chances he had of getting out of this alive depended upon keeping himself under strict discipline, upon not letting them sense the slightest fear or uncertainty in him.

Coming out of the trees, he saw them, five in all, gathered around the cow-camp corral. Shorty Hough was among them.

Twenty-Four

Smoke rising from the tin chimney of the cabin told Kirk they had been here overnight. Shorty Hough was inside the corral roping out a horse. The others had already caught and saddled their mounts. Eli Yockey was with them. He was the first to see Kirk when he rode out of the timber.

Eli grabbed for the rifle on his saddle, then changed his mind. He said nothing, but the others, following his gaze, saw Kirk while he was still twenty-five yards away.

Now Kirk neither hurried nor slowed his horse. This was the dangerous time; this was the moment when guilt and fear, or plain nervousness, could stampede these men into taking almost any action. They kept looking behind him as though expecting to see the Tomahawk crew ride out of the trees.

"You thieving murderers," Kirk said, his voice steady. "The first one of you that touches a gun is dead."

Eli's hands were shaking so badly that he stuffed them into his pockets. He said shakily, "Kirk, about Delfino and Matt . . ."

"Shut your mouth," Kirk said savagely.

Still astride his mount, Kirk looked over the corral fence at Shorty Hough. The horses were milling around in a circle. Each time a horse passed between Kirk and Shorty, either man had time to draw without being seen. Tension built up in Kirk.

"Come out of there, Shorty," he said. "I'm going to kill you. I'm giving you more chance than you gave Delfino and Matt."

Shorty looked at Eli and the others, his glance compelling. They shifted and moved, but now that they'd passed up their initial chance to end this by killing Kirk, they carefully kept their hands clear of their guns.

Shorty's face tightened. Kirk's mount fidgeted. His right hand hung suspended above the grips of his gun. The horses in the corral continued to mill, but at the moment all of them were on the far side. In another instant they'd pass in front of Shorty, and Kirk knew that when the last one had gone by, Shorty's gun would be in his hand.

Hugging the fence, the horses completed the circle of the corral, going in front of Shorty. He moved an instant before they shut him off from view, his hand speeding toward his gun.

Kirk vaulted from the back of his horse. His gun was in his hand as his feet touched the ground. He stumbled on a rock and staggered, but recovered just as the last of the horses thundered past. The poles of the corral were between him and Shorty, whose gun was lined on the place where he had last seen Kirk.

Pure panic showed in Shorty's face for an instant, then he saw Kirk standing on the ground. He fired anxiously, too swiftly, before his gun had come to bear on Kirk.

Kirk raised his gun to eye level, the only way he could be sure his bullet would not be deflected by one of the corral poles. Shorty slammed another shot at him, this one striking a pole at waist height and showering Kirk with splinters.

Kirk lined his sights on Shorty and squeezed off his shot. Shorty fired again, but it was shock that had pulled the trigger. He staggered back a full step, recovered, and lined his sights on Kirk again.

Following him with the muzzle of his gun, Kirk threw another shot, apprehensive of the others behind him and to one side; unless he got Shorty at once, they'd jump into it, something they had been afraid to do while Kirk was in position to watch them.

Kirk's second shot drove Shorty back like the kick of a horse's hoof. His legs pumped frantically as he tried to keep himself erect, and failed. His shoulders slammed into one of the milling horses and the animal whirled and lashed out with both hind feet. They caught Shorty as he was falling and lifted him like a broken doll, flinging him into the middle of the corral where he fell to lie twisted and still.

Kirk wheeled, his gun ready, the hammer back. He caught Eli Yockey in the act of raising his rifle to his shoulder. One of the others had a hand on the butt of his revolver. Kirk snapped a shot over their heads. Eli lowered his rifle. The other man's hand dropped away from his holstered revolver.

"Hold it," Kirk said. They froze and he went on, "Now get in there and load Shorty on one of your animals. Tie him down and make it fast or I'm likely to forget I don't want to kill you."

They moved with speed, glancing at him often and uneasily. They hoisted Shorty over a saddle and tied him down.

Kirk mounted his horse and took the reins of Shorty's from the shaken Eli. He said, "Get off Tomahawk range. I don't know any reason why I should except that I feel sorry for your cows, but I'll lease you Tomahawk grass for the summer. The price is two-bits a head. Send me your tallies along with the money to cover the lease. Don't show your faces on our grass till roundup in the fall. Don't ever try taking anything from Tomahawk again."

They didn't reply, but he didn't expect them to. He swung his horse and trailing Shorty's with the lifeless burden, galloped back in the direction he had come. Fear for the Tomahawk crew turned him cold. If he had taken too long, and was too late. . . .

His horse was nearly finished when he heard the sound of firing ahead. He spurred, demanding and getting the last shred of the horse's strength. He rode directly into the ravine, into plain sight without making any effort to seek cover.

Salt Creek re-inforcements had the Tomahawk men surrounded now, just as Tomahawk had surrounded the original party of invaders. They were pouring a murderous fire into Surrency's men, driving them slowly into the hollow.

Kirk turned in his saddle and pointed at Shorty's limp body. "He's dead!" he shouted at them. "So get off Tomahawk before it happens to you, too!"

It was a reckless gamble; he could not watch all of them, and it would have been easy enough for one of the hidden Salt Creek men to knock him out of his saddle. But he knew how much they had depended on Shorty, how much of their courage and greed had come from him.

The firing halted abruptly. A minute later Lew Warren called, "All right, Kirk. We're pullin' out." A minute or so later they began their retreat, silently, keeping under cover as much as they could.

Frank Surrency stood up from behind a down log. The

rest of the crew stood up, too, staring defiantly at the retreating Salt Creekers. There was no more firing.

Surrency approached and Kirk said, "I'm going to lease them range, Frank. At two-bits a head for the summer."

Surrency nodded as if he understood. Suddenly tired, Kirk handed him the reins of Shorty's horse. "Maybe they'll want to bury him," he said, and turning, rode toward home.

He saw Bianca coming from a long way off. She rode like an Indian girl, bareback, with only a length of rope for a hackamore. With the end of it, she was beating her horse's rump mercilessly. The animal was in a dead run, leaping brush, dodging trees, sailing over gullies and washouts. Bianca clung to his back like a burr, her hair whipping out behind her.

Kirk waved to her, and she saw him and swung her horse toward him. When she reached him, she pulled her plunging mount to a halt. Her eyes sparkled with anger.

"Damn that Frank Surrency! He ran the horses out, and it took me all this time to . . ."

Tears were close. Tenderness and relief were just under the surface of her fury. Kirk swung off his horse and went to her. He held his arms up.

"Come here. You think I want to wait forever?"

She was off her horse and into his arms, fiercely eager. He kissed her, long and hard, the way he had wanted to last night.

He said, "Get up on my horse. We'd better find a preacher and keep you an honest woman."

Her eyes shone but she said nothing. She didn't need to. Her eyes gave him all the promise a man could ever want.

Ballantine brings you the best of the West— And the best western authors

Ride into the world of adventure with Ballantine's western novels!